the secret of Luca

Ignazio Silone

the secret of Luca

TRANSLATED BY DARINA SILONE

HARPER & BROTHERS, NEW YORK

the secret of Luca

CHAPTER ONE

IT HAD been a stiff climb up the rocky goat track. The old man's pace, as he approached the top, was slow but even. The track leveled out again into the winding dirt road at a point where a great iron crucifix rose from a stone pedestal. Here the man paused for a moment, to recover his wind and wipe the sweat from his face.

A woman huddled on the ground behind the cross. She was a young peasant, dressed in black, with a white kerchief on her head. It was hard to tell whether she was resting or praying. At her side lay a big basket of red peppers. On the pedestal of the cross were engraved the words:

IN MEMORY OF THE LENTEN MISSION
OF THE PASSIONIST FATHERS
A.D. 1900

The man stared at the inscription. Presently, the woman noticed him.

"Where are you from?" she asked. But the man did not

1

answer. He looked to be about seventy and very poor, but he was nonetheless a fine, tall, strong fellow, obviously still able to work, although of no identifiable trade. An odd thing about him, in that district, was that his head was bare. His gray hair was cropped short, he had several days' growth of beard, and he was barefoot. His clothes were clean, but patched and frayed. Thick and heavy, they seemed strangely unsuited to the season. A long loaf of white bread and a pair of shoes protruded from the sack he carried slung across his shoulder.

The woman felt for a coin in the pocket of her skirt and offered it to the stranger. "Go on," she said, "take it." He glanced at her outstretched hand in great embarrassment.

"Oh, no," he murmured. "Thanks all the same. But there's no need."

"I didn't mean to offend you," she apologized. Then she tried again: "Have you come a long way? Do you know the country hereabouts?"

The man didn't answer, as though he had not heard, and began to walk off. But confronted for the first time with a full view of the mountain, he stopped in his tracks.

"What happened?" he exclaimed, turning to the woman. "Where's the forest?"

"Didn't you know?" she asked. He shook his head emphatically. In front of him, black and naked, the mountain reared itself into a great hump on which a few wan, palsied shrubs were growing.

"Did they burn it down?" Sadness and horror mingled in his face. "Was it the war?"

2

"No," said the woman. "No one knows how it happened. Some say it was God's curse."

"When did it happen?"

The woman thought for a while.

"I don't recall the year, nor the season," she answered finally. "I just remember that it was a Friday."

"There's been many a Friday in all these years," said the man, his eyes still fixed on the bleak ridge of the mountain.

"Yes, of course," the woman admitted, "but isn't it always the same Friday?"

The man trudged forward again, following the narrow road that had been carved out of the mountainside. He rounded the first bend and there lay the village, straight ahead of him, spreadeagled on the slope of a hill. A tall signpost bore its name:

CISTERNA DEI MARSI
Altitude 3,088 feet above sea level

Little fields of burnt stubble, dotted with a few meager almond trees and blackberry bushes, now flanked the road on both sides. Before reaching the foot of the hill it crossed a stone bridge beneath which a stream flowed in a steep-sided bed. The man made his way down to the bank by a path of rough-hewn steps and looked about for a clean place to put his sack down.

Directly below the bridge, the stream plunged from an overhanging ledge of stone to form a deep, limpid pool.

The man sat down on a patch of grass at the edge of the bank and let the water lap around his tired, dusty feet. He seemed to enjoy the icy current, for he promptly began to kick and splash with the liveliness of a boy. Once, for a moment, he shut his eyes and smiled. He dried his feet in the sun afterward, and fetched the shoes from his sack, but he had something of a struggle when it came to getting them on. His other ablutions, rinsing hands, face and neck, were quickly dealt with. Then he prepared to quench his thirst. He flung himself full length on the bank and leaned out over the stream, bending down till the water touched his face. He drank in long draughts, the way a horse drinks at the end of a hard day's work. He was back on his feet again, mopping his face, when he heard a shout. The man lying on the grass a few yards away in the shade of an acacia had until that moment escaped his notice.

"There's a public fountain," this man told him. "If you want to drink, there's a fountain as you go into the village."

"Oh, so now you have a fountain?"

"Where are you from?" the other asked, curious. "Are you looking for someone?"

But the stranger, all of a sudden, seemed to be in a hurry. Without answering, he climbed back to the road and proceeded steadily up the hill to the outskirts of the village.

Plunged in its deathlike afternoon torpor, the village seemed uninhabited. The streets were deserted, the doors

4

and windows closed and silent. Neat, newly built little houses, the mortar scarcely dry on them, fronted the main street side by side with ancient dwellings, squalid makeshift huts, and crumbling piles of masonry.

Inside the precincts of the village the stranger's pace became erratic, quickening nervously, then slackening, or even halting abruptly. At one spot where a group of houses had collapsed into a rubble heap he stood for a while, gazing up at the vanished windows and balconies. He walked down the middle of the street in a blinding glare of sunlight, unseen and unheard in that solitude of ruins and walls. It was as though he were some ghostly visitor, some uneasy spirit.

When he got to the old church he hesitated for a moment, then went round to the parish house. A man lay sprawled among the flies and dust on the threshold, blocking the stranger's access to the doorbell. His scanty covering of rags revealed a black, wizened body, like a charred corpse. But the stranger's shadow falling on him was enough to wake him.

"What brings you here at this hour?" the sleeper mumbled fretfully, his eyes half shut.

"I'd like to see the parish priest."

A look of mild exasperation crossed the man's face.

"How often do I have to tell you," he muttered, "that we only give charity on Fridays?"

The stranger insisted: "Can't I see the parish priest?"

"Don Franco's asleep at this hour," he whined. "Everyone's asleep."

The stranger seemed puzzled.

5

"What did you say the parish priest's name is?"

"His name's Don Franco, if that's all right with you."

"Oh, then I'm sorry I disturbed you. He's not the man I was looking for."

The stranger made his way back around the church and plunged into the maze of crooked alleys, narrow as corridors, that made up the oldest part of the village. Each step sounded on the cobblestones like the footfall of a night prowler. Suddenly, in the silence, there was the clatter of shutters flung open on the first-floor balcony of an old house. A tall, gaunt, black-garbed woman groped blindly out to the railing and bent her face, with its empty eye sockets, toward the approaching steps.

"Whose step is that?" she cried piercingly. "Man, I can hear you."

The footsteps died away instantly. The man stopped dead in the middle of the lane to stare at the apparition.

"Is it you?" Now the woman's tone was pleading, anxious. She called out several times. "Is it you?"

But then a girl came and began coaxing her gently back into the house.

"It's a tramp," the girl said. "It's only a tramp."

"Beware of false tramps," shrieked the blind woman, unconvinced.

The man didn't move until he saw the balcony shutters close again; then he resumed his way, but with a softer tread this time, almost on tiptoe. He did not have to go much farther to reach his goal. It was a little square, surrounded on three sides by rubble; on the fourth there stood the ruined shell of a modest house. The door was barred by a wooden plank nailed horizontally across the two leaves, and one wall of the only remaining upper story had collapsed, leaving the interior at the mercy of the weather and the weeds.

The man put down his sack and began wrenching and heaving at the plank that barred the door. But the plank was of hard wood, chestnut or beech, and the nails were big and rusted and had been driven in deep.

"You're wasting your time."

The voice startled him, coming from right behind him.

"I know what the inside's like," it went on gaily. "There's nothing left to steal."

The owner of the voice turned out to be a small, shirtless, barefooted urchin, with tousled hair and short pants held up by string. He must have emerged from one of the nearby rubble heaps; his face was the same grimy color as the rubble.

The man made several more attempts to break down the door, hitting it hard with his shoulder.

"What you need is an iron bar," said the boy, holding something behind his back as he spoke.

"An iron bar, yes," said the man, "but how am I going to find one?"

"If you'll make friends with me," said the boy, "I'll give you mine"; he produced the object he had been hiding.

"Thanks," said the man, beginning to get interested. "Tell me, what's your name?"

"Toni. And yours?"

"Luca. Who's your father?"

"I don't know. They call me Pighead."

The man smiled.

"Well, I don't want to boast," he said, "nor compare myself to you, but that's what they used to call me when I was your age."

Toni burst out laughing, furrowing the mask of mud on his face. There was a precocious gleam of shrewdness and sagacity in his strange green eyes.

"Are you good at being friends?" he asked the man in a solemn tone. "Can you keep a promise?"

"I think so."

"Can you keep a secret?"

"Yes, Toni, I think I can. Any more questions?"

"That'll do for the present. Come on, let's get going before they all wake up."

CHAPTER TWO

"I'LL BE with you right away," the mayor told the delegation of war veterans waiting in the corridor outside his office. "Can't you be patient? I'll only be a minute or two."

"You mean that cop gets priority over us?" one of the veterans protested.

The mayor forced his pale, suety face into a smile. Then he closed the door and went back to his desk. The sergeant in command of the local police force was still slumped in a chair beside it, pulling at his collar.

"Did you hear them?" the mayor complained. "I haven't been in this job for a month, and I'm fed up with it already."

"Yes, it's tiring work, serving the people," the sergeant agreed. His tone was faintly caustic. "What do they want now?"

"They want to get out of here," the mayor muttered. "They want to emigrate."

Through the open window waves of heat surged as from the mouth of a furnace.

"Can't we shut that window?" the sergeant implored.

"Mustn't keep out the fresh air," the mayor told him. "Want me to order you a lemonade?"

"Do you call that fresh air?" the sergeant protested.

The mayor himself, however, for all his youth and burly frame, not only looked exhausted, but had lost his bounce.

"Mind if I take these off?" he asked, removing his coat and tie and flinging them on the typewriter. A dripping shirt, transparent with sweat and too tight for him, encased the fleshy expanse of his chest like butcher's paper. The general effect was porcine, and the sergeant eyed him with distaste.

"Oh, by the way," the mayor said, "that affair you were mentioning—I really can't be bothered with it. It's not even in my bailiwick."

"Which affair? Perhaps I haven't made myself clear—"

"I mean the case of that fellow, what's his name? The one that's getting out of jail."

"The penitentiary," the sergeant amended.

"It's all the same to me. I can't be bothered. His crime wasn't political."

"It wasn't political and it wasn't criminal," said the sergeant. "You know as well as I do why they're releasing him. They've found out he's innocent."

"Very well, I'll give his name to the parish welfare committee," said the mayor. "Isn't that enough? We'll have one more beggar on our hands."

"The welfare committee won't help maintain law and order," observed the sergeant.

"Law and order? Would you mind explaining how law and order can possibly be endangered by the return of an innocent man? What do you want them to do—leave him in the penitentiary?"

"You're not being very co-operative," said the sergeant dryly. "If you like we can postpone the discussion till this evening, when it's cooler."

"You find me stupid, eh?" The mayor giggled. "No, don't go, please sit down again. Explain your point of view properly. Look here, do let me get you a lemonade."

"I was referring to the effect that the mere announcement of this man's return has already produced on the people of the village," the sergeant explained. "It can't have escaped your notice."

"Oh, come off it. Who remembers him? It's a good forty years since he was convicted. Who'd know him now?"

"The old people know him," said the sergeant. "Didn't you see the way the old people reacted to the news?"

"You're right, I hadn't thought about it—this is an old folks' village. Well, what did the old folks say?"

"Nothing—that's what's so serious. They're so scared they won't even talk."

"Our old folks aren't very talkative at the best of times. It's hard to tell what their silence means. They can make you think that they're plotting the most frightful things, when the odds are they're just woolgathering! How can you tell?"

There was a violent and prolonged bout of hammering on the door.

"Just a minute," the mayor shouted in exasperation.

"Well, I'll get out of the way," said the sergeant, getting to his feet.

"No, you won't," said the mayor. "Those fellows can

wait. Unemployed veterans aren't that pressed for time. So please sit down again and tell me frankly what it is you're afraid of."

"The thing that worries me in the old people isn't so much their silence," the sergeant explained. "It's the way they begin to shuffle and look sideways the instant anyone mentions that man—remind me of his name, will you?"

The mayor hacked a path through the jungle of papers on his desk.

"Luca Sabatini," he said. "Now tell me honestly what it is you suspect. Were there false witnesses at his trial?"

The sergeant nodded.

"That's my hunch," he said, "more or less."

"In short, you're afraid this Sabatini may be coming back bent on—h'm—revenge?"

"Humanly speaking," said the sergeant, "it would be understandable. Put yourself in his shoes."

"No, thanks," said the mayor, "I prefer my own. But even supposing these false witnesses had ever existed, wouldn't they be dead by now? Let's hope they are, anyway. How many years ago did it all happen?"

"I wish I could be certain of it," said the sergeant. "And in any case, what guarantee do we have that he won't take revenge on their children?"

"You needn't ask me—I tell you, I know nothing about it," the mayor exclaimed, losing his patience. "All these suppositions are getting us nowhere. I wasn't even born when the trial took place—that much at least I can prove pretty easily. Most people were even beginning to forget about it by the time I was a kid. Incidentally—this is be-

12

tween ourselves, of course—my father was convinced the fellow was guilty."

"By the way," remarked the sergeant, "wasn't your father one of the witnesses for the prosecution?"

"I've no idea. What makes you ask that? What are you trying to insinuate?"

"Or anyway your late father-in-law? One never knows. . . ."

"You're crazy," cried the mayor. "No, sorry, don't get up, you can't possibly go just yet. After all, we've got to decide on something."

"We'd better think fast, then," said the sergeant.

"If you like," the mayor suggested, "I could try and get one of the old men to talk. It'll cost me a few bottles of wine, of course. . . ."

"And it might help," added the sergeant, "if some reliable person could sound out this unfortunate wretch, the moment he shows up, so as to find out what frame of mind he's in, what his next move is likely to be—that sort of thing."

"Well, who's your idea of a reliable person? The standard's pretty low these days."

"I was thinking of Don Franco," said the sergeant. "As a matter of fact, I've already got in touch with him about it—"

The mayor pulled a face.

"I don't think Don Franco's very suitable," he remarked. "He's too young—barely my age. And anyway he's only interested in public works these days. He missed his vocation. He should have been a contractor."

13

"If that's how it is," said the sergeant, "why don't you have a word yourself with the other priest—the old one, what's his name?"

"Don Serafino," said the mayor. "Yes, I think he'd probably be the right person. But I'm not the one to approach him, I'm afraid. We haven't been on nodding— let alone speaking—terms for some time. Oh, you don't know him, sergeant. You've no idea how tiresome and indiscreet that old priest can be. Well, it's a long story, but to put it in a nutshell, he just won't stick to his professional duties. He's not content with telling women and children to believe in God—he actually believes it all himself. You think I'm just being funny, don't you? Or exaggerating, anyway. Well, I'm not. I give you my solemn oath that I have it straight from his own lips: he still believes in the existence of God. Fancy that."

"And Don Franco," said the sergeant, "you think he doesn't. . . ."

"Don Franco," the mayor assured him, "believes in nothing but the Ministry of Public Works. Why, only the other day . . ."

"Very well, then," the sergeant broke in, "I'll try talking to Don Serafino myself. We've no time to lose."

The mayor was suddenly anxious.

"What are you hinting at?" he demanded. "You mean that fellow's likely to turn up in Cisterna at any moment?"

"I showed you the official letter, didn't I?" the sergeant said. "It's a matter of a few days, at the outside."

"I've so many headaches," the mayor said plaintively, "and this is the last straw."

14

He saw the sergeant to the door. The janitor sprang to attention, cap in one hand and pipe in the other. The corridor was empty.

"What's become of the veterans?" the mayor wanted to know.

"They got tired of waiting, your honor," the janitor replied. "They gave me a message for you, only I'd best not repeat it. It's not very respectful. But of course if your honor insists . . ."

"Where did they go?"

"To party headquarters, your honor."

"Here come my troubles," muttered the mayor to himself, slamming the door of his office in a thoroughly bad temper.

The sergeant kept his promise to the mayor and lost no time in trying to find Don Serafino, but his search was fruitless. The old priest was neither at home nor in church, nor was he sitting in the shade in any of his favorite spots. Without a word of explanation to his housekeeper, and at an hour when the streets were deserted, he had taken his ancient gray cotton umbrella and slipped out of the parish house. Had he been summoned to a deathbed? Someone would have heard about it.

The stifling afternoon hours dragged slowly by. But no sooner had the church bell rung for Vespers than doors and windows that had been shut against the heat of the day began to open, artisans brought their work tables out into the street, and peasant women waiting for their husbands to come home from the fields resumed their gossip

15

from one threshold to another.

There was no sign of the priest, however, until just before the Angelus. Then a donkey with a load of corn came ambling down the path from the crest of the hill above the village, followed by an old peasant and, beside him, the priest. The peasant was a certain Ludovico, a former miller, and a very strange man. From the day he had been forced out of business by the town's new electric mill (though that may not have been the only reason), he had lapsed into a black melancholy from which nothing could rouse him.

But even Don Serafino's gaunt, austere face showed an unaccustomed preoccupation. It would have been hard to guess what the two men were talking about. The former parish priest and the former miller were among the oldest inhabitants of the village, and when old people get together no one else can understand them. Now, however, the two old men were silent even though they continued to walk side by side, as if they had nothing left to say to each other.

They had reached San Bartolommeo's crossing, and were about to separate, when Don Serafino clutched Ludovico by the arm, leaving the donkey to wander on by itself toward the stable.

"Don't be so stubborn. Listen to me," the priest said.

"Let me alone," Ludovico muttered.

"One of these days he'll be coming back. We can't refuse to see him and help him."

"I don't know whom you're talking about; let go," Ludovico repeated, a glint of hatred in his eyes.

16

"I'm not going to find it any too easy myself, let me tell you," Don Serafino assured him. "But it was all so long ago. Now he's an old man too."

The miller stood there with his head hanging down, like a donkey, his arms limp, his mouth half open, and stared at the ground. Suddenly his fury exploded.

"Don't make me blaspheme," he shouted at the priest. "Let me go."

But Don Serafino would not resign himself to defeat.

"We're among the few people still alive who can remember the catastrophe," he said in a voice strangled with emotion. "We were his friends. Have you forgotten?"

Ludovico wrenched his arm free from Don Serafino's grasp and started running clumsily in pursuit of his donkey. For a while the priest stood watching him; then he continued with slow, weary steps, leaning on his umbrella as though it were a cane, until he reached the little square facing the church of San Bartolommeo. Here he spied the sergeant, still some distance away, and, in the hope of avoiding him, sat down on one of the stone seats built into the façade of the church.

This church, half demolished by the last earthquake and never restored, was no longer used as a place of worship. A segment of the dome still soared above what was left of the walls; and across the violet sky of its painted ceiling, a band of angels wafted festoons of roses and white ribbons inscribed in golden letters GLORIA GLORIA GLORIA. The square was deserted, but its two rows of dusty little trees were alive with clamoring cicadas. A small brown donkey with enormous ears was standing motionless,

17

tethered to one of the trees. The sergeant bore down on the priest.

"Is something the matter?" he asked. "You don't look well."

"It's nothing serious," the priest told him. "I get a little short of breath in the evenings, just about sundown."

"Well, in that case," said the sergeant, "maybe you'd prefer to see me tomorrow morning? It's really rather urgent, though."

"What is it?" the priest inquired.

The sergeant sat down beside him on the stone bench.

"I wonder," he said, "if you remember Luca Sabatini. He was a parishioner of yours many years ago. Do you happen to remember him?"

"Yes, it must have been many years ago." The priest spoke as if the words were being dragged out of him. "A great many years ago, before the recent catastrophes."

"He was the victim, as we all know," the sergeant pursued, "of a deplorable miscarriage of justice. Now he's coming back, and I won't pretend to you that I'm not worried. Of course you realize that I'm speaking in the interest of the whole community. I was just wondering if you happen to remember who the witnesses were whose testimony led to his conviction?"

"How should I remember?" The priest seemed genuinely astonished. "I was never concerned with anything except my parish duties. In this village people mind their own business."

"Naturally." The sergeant smiled. "But perhaps you can at least recall whether or not any villagers did testify against Sabatini—even in good faith, I mean?"

"I know nothing about it," said the priest hastily. He was obviously upset. "As I've already told you, I don't remember anything."

"Of course not." The sergeant's laugh was faintly sardonic. "I didn't expect you would. But perhaps I haven't made myself clear. What I meant was, now that Luca's innocence has been established, one can't help wondering why he didn't find some way of proving it at the trial."

The priest no longer attempted to conceal his irritation.

"Why ask me?" he retorted with a shrug. But the sergeant was used to being patient. He said:

"A while back the mayor and I were talking to someone in the village. I gather that Sabatini didn't even try to defend himself at the trial."

The priest nodded resignedly.

"I have heard that too," he said. "No, he didn't defend himself."

"The most damaging piece of evidence," the sergeant went on, "appears to have been the fact that Sabatini wasn't home on the night of the murder, and that in court he refused to tell where he had spent the time."

"He didn't defend himself," the priest agreed. "That much I heard, all right. But I assure you I know nothing more."

"No one else came forward to reveal whatever he was hiding?"

"No one."

"Forgive me, your reverence," said the sergeant, "but the whole thing seems improbable."

"Truth," said the priest, "often seems improbable."

"To come back to the present," said the sergeant, "can you honestly say that you're not in the least uneasy at the prospect of Luca's return?"

The priest was silent for a long moment. When he finally answered, his voice was very faint. "It would be a lie to deny it."

"Tell me," the sergeant pursued, "do you feel there's anything specific to be afraid of? Might he have been hiding some deep resentment behind his mysterious behavior at the trial?"

"I don't know," the priest replied. "I feel an anxiety that I can't put into words. He's innocent, and therefore he has a right to his liberty. But what can he do with it here? The world he knew is dead and gone. For myself and the handful of others old enough to remember him, this meeting is going to be like a reunion with a ghost. . . . But forgive me, these are selfish considerations. There's the practical aspect: what's Luca going to live on when he gets back? Is the state going to pay him any compensation for his years of unjust imprisonment?"

"There's no legal provision for it," the sergeant said.

"You mean there's no provision for judicial errors?"

"The state," explained the sergeant, "recognizes no legal obligation to recompense the victims of judicial errors. Doesn't Luca have any relatives? Doesn't he have any property?"

"None," said the priest.

While the conversation between priest and sergeant drew to its close, a barefooted ragamuffin entered the square,

20

wearing an army jacket that flapped about his knees, and kicking an old milk can in front of him with a hideous noise.

"Toni," Don Serafino called out, "you'll hurt your feet."

Toni promptly abandoned the can and, feigning a limp, hobbled over to sit down beside the priest.

"I've just had an idea," said Don Serafino, turning back to the sergeant. "Before Luca gets here, couldn't they arrange to put him in the county home? It seems to me the poor fellow would meet all the necessary requirements."

"That's a lucky inspiration," the sergeant told him. "You must have got it straight from Providence. I'll have a word with the mayor at once."

Scarcely had the sergeant disappeared behind the church when Toni murmured: "I came to bring you some news I thought you'd be very glad to hear."

"What news?" the priest inquired eagerly.

"Oh, now it doesn't matter," said the boy, sulking.

"Come on, tell me, what news?"

Toni whispered something into the priest's ear, and saw his unexpectedly troubled look.

"He's here already?" Don Serafino exclaimed. "Since when?"

"Since yesterday."

"Where is he?"

"I don't know that it's right to tell you. Oh, well, he's at home."

"Among the ruins."

"I got him a pallet, and some odds and ends."

21

"Has anyone seen him?"

"So far he hasn't wanted to be seen."

"Did he send you to find me?"

"He doesn't want to be seen, he told me, until he finds out about the village, who's alive, who's dead, that sort of thing. But how could I answer his questions? I don't know much about him, even. All I know is, he's not an ordinary sort of man. So then I offered to go and bring some old friend to see him. But he couldn't think of anybody. 'There used to be a priest here,' he said, 'a priest called Don Serafino. In fact,' he said, 'as soon as I got here I went looking for him at the sacristy, but from what they told me I think he must be dead.' So then I explained to him that you weren't the parish priest any longer on account of being old, but that you weren't dead at all. You should have seen how pleased he was to hear that! But you—you want to have him locked up all over again. I oughtn't ever to have told you he was back—I can see that now. I was an idiot to trust you."

Toni went no further because he saw that Don Serafino's eyes had filled with tears.

"Let's go," the priest said, rising abruptly to his feet. "Take me to him."

The boy turned a handspring to show his delight. He had the pliant grace of a young willow tree.

"We'd better not walk together," he said. "It's a bit risky. Anyhow, you know the way."

CHAPTER THREE

Don Serafino's study was dark, sepulchral. On a table covered with a faded and wax-spattered green baize cloth, the principal object, standing between two wooden candlesticks and several black-bound prayerbooks, was a skull—a real human skull.

"More coffee?" inquired Don Serafino.

"No, thanks," Luca said.

"A biscuit?"

"No, thanks. But I'd like to take Toni a few, if you have a piece of paper."

The old priest rose at once to prepare the little parcel. He was tall, ascetically thin, with a long angular chin, narrow pointed nose and hollow cheeks. His hands, shriveled with age and gnarled with arthritis, looked like the claws of an old rooster. Just then a shaft of sunlight fell from one of the tiny windows, and a million particles of dust began to dance down the luminous ribbon that cleft the room in two.

"Andrea Cipriani is expected here tomorrow," Don Serafino said. "You couldn't have known him; he's not yet forty. I don't know how many or exactly what misdeeds he has perpetrated in the last few years. All I know is that he's acquired a red halo as a revolutionary leader. This'll be his first time back in Cisterna, and since the revolutionary cause has prevailed in the meanwhile, they're not going to arrest him—they're going to carry him in triumph."

"I've heard about him," Luca said. "Isn't he Carmine's son?"

"Yes, he's the son of your friend Carmine," the priest answered. "You remember Carmine? He was a man who accepted the established order, but his son chose to live the hard way, and the times have given him plenty of scope."

"As usual, I learned of Carmine's death by accident and long after it had happened," Luca said. "I felt as though I'd lost a brother. I don't know whether any two boys were ever as close as we were. Later, in my last years as a free man, we drifted apart. He had gotten married and I had become involved in difficulties he would not have understood. But I think he always wished me well."

"Much more than that, I can assure you," the priest said. "He suffered a great deal during your trial. He kept coming to me, imploring me to explain why you were behaving so absurdly. But what could I say to him?"

"I know, too, that he supported and helped my mother until the day she died," Luca said. "She mentioned it in every letter."

"Why not let me put your case to Andrea?" asked Don Serafino. "I don't think you need feel any false pride where

24

he's concerned. He's an influential man now; he might be able to get you a decent pension."

"Then you really believe I can't find work?"

"I tell you, it's next to impossible. Even the young people can't find work."

"I'd like to see Andrea," Luca said, "even if it's only for a moment, just long enough to shake hands."

"Tomorrow will be difficult," said the priest. "It's his first time back in Cisterna, don't forget. He'll be busy with the officials and his party comrades."

"You mean he has supporters even in Cisterna?"

"So I gather. The winner always has supporters."

"Is it true that he, too, has been in prison?"

"Yes, for a few months, and, later, he was on a penal island for several years."

"It's a mystery to me," Luca said. "How did Andrea manage to discover politics in a place like Cisterna?"

"Politics, my dear Luca, is like cholera now," Don Serafino explained. "And a bacillus, once it begins to spread, is hard to keep track of. Andrea, to all appearances, was simply a schoolmaster—and good at his job, so people used to say, in spite of his contrary and difficult temperament. To tell you the truth, though, he was eccentric even as a boy. His mother used to come and talk to me about his odd behavior, asking my advice. Had he been a girl, I'd have said he was hysterical. But nobody could have foreseen the outcome. It was so unexpected. At the beginning of one of those campaigns the late government used to launch against defenseless peoples (I forget now whose turn it was, the Spaniards' or the Ethiopians'), Andrea announced to some acquaintances in the public square: 'It's an outrage.' The scandal lay not so much in what he'd actually said, as in the fact that he'd said it in public. He could have denied saying it and gotten out of it. But he did just the opposite, as though he'd been waiting all along for just such an opportunity. Summoned to party headquarters, he repeated his statement and, apparently, added to it. Obviously, it was more than enough justification for them to clap him into prison and all the rest. Now in recent years . . ."

Someone kept knocking at the door.

"Who is it?" said Don Serafino.

The town hall janitor appeared in the doorway. Visibly taken aback at seeing Luca, he proceeded, after one sidelong glance, to ignore him.

"What do you want?" the priest inquired.

"Don Serafino," said the janitor, "the mayor wants to see you. He says it's urgent."

"What for?"

"Beg pardon, but I wasn't told the reason."

"Who has given your mayor the right to summon me, as if I were one of his garbage men?"

"You don't seem to have heard the latest about the garbage men," said the janitor with a grin. "They're not at his beck and call any longer. They've been on strike since yesterday. Haven't you noticed the stink in the streets?"

"Oh," said the priest, "I thought it was just a natural consequence of the new mayor."

The janitor laughed scornfully.

"Can I tell him you said that?" he asked. "You know it would please me a lot. About his wanting to see you, maybe I can guess the reason. At the town hall they're trying to get up a committee for tomorrow's reception in honor of Andrea Cipriani."

"What do they want me for? Let them ask the parish priest."

"Maybe they feel they could do with your advice as a friend of the great man," the janitor suggested.

Luca gave Don Serafino a nudge.

"If I were you," he said in an undertone, "I wouldn't stand back—not this time. You might be able to spare Andrea some annoyance."

"Very well." Don Serafino gave a sigh of resignation. "I'll come, but not till later. At present I have a guest."

"You don't seem to have a very high opinion of the new mayor," Luca remarked, chuckling, when the janitor had departed.

"He's an odd sort of freethinker," Don Serafino explained. "The poor fellow's convinced that freethinking is really free fornication."

A number of dignitaries—the mayor and the town clerk, the parish priest Don Franco, and the new members of the town council, two of them artisans, one a peasant—had gathered in the town hall to discuss the program for the following day. They were waiting for Don Serafino, but when he failed to appear they briefly exchanged views among themselves.

The mayor said: "The theme of the ceremony should be

27

approximately as follows: 'Cisterna welcomes her most illustrious son.' What do you think?" he asked Don Franco. "How does it strike you?"

The parish priest—plump, squat and, although still quite young, almost completely bald—was sitting at the window, enjoying the cool evening air. He confined himself to a smile.

"I'll have my say later on," he said. "How's that garbage strike coming along?"

The mayor turned to the town clerk.

"How about you?" he asked.

The town clerk was a thin, swarthy, bespectacled man with an almost greenish complexion. He was at that moment intent on checking accounts in a big ledger, and took no notice of the mayor's question.

The three newly appointed councilors sat formal and shy on a settee beside the mayor's desk, consulting one another with furtive glances. The oldest of the three—a wizened little man, all skin and bones—was obviously very poor, his clothes being mostly patches. He apologized for bringing up a question of good breeding, as he expressed it.

"Don't you think," he explained, "that we should speak to the people who informed on Signor Cipriani and got him arrested? Oughtn't we to drop them a sort of friendly hint to stay away from the reception?"

"Er—yes, of course," the mayor muttered. "What do you both think?" he asked the priest and the town clerk.

"My dear fellow," the town clerk began, looking up from his ledger, "Once you start . . . " But he broke off. He

28

had a way, when speaking, of jerking his head backward, as though expecting a slap.

"Well, never mind," he concluded, "you see what I mean. . . ."

The councilor was gaining confidence. "Oughtn't we to keep out the people who signed the petition disqualifying Cipriani as a schoolteacher? What do you think?"

"It seems so to me," said another councilor.

That much was obvious. But the roster of undesirables was still incomplete.

"What about the ones who threw stones at him when they saw him handcuffed to the policemen?" added the old man. "I don't know if any of you remember that. I just happened to be there. I was on my way back from the mill, with my donkey. . . ."

Another councilor had been there too and remembered the scene. "Stop that," one of the policemen had shouted. "You might hit one of us."

The tale was heard in silence. It was embarrassing to discuss these matters. But at a certain moment the town clerk again raised his head from his ledger and said with a grim smile: "If we're going to exclude all the unworthy ones, may I ask who'll be left to attend the reception? A handful of ignorant peasants, maybe, but no respectable people at all. Well, am I right?"

After a few painful moments of reflection the mayor decided that there would be no discrimination against anyone.

"We're living in a democracy now," he announced. "Democracy means equality, doesn't it?"

But the formula that quelled every scruple, including perhaps even the oldest councilor's, was the one evolved by Don Franco.

"Andrea Cipriani," he said, speaking slowly and solemnly, "must surely know, in his present exalted position, that the best revenge is forgiveness."

The mayor felt that the phrase hit the nail exactly on the head, and after getting Don Franco to repeat it, he copied it out on a piece of paper to incorporate it in his speech the next day.

"And if you want to make it sound even better still," the town clerk suggested in a whisper, "tell them Garibaldi said it. That will bring the house down."

The mayor felt that all the really important questions had now been settled, subject to the approval of Don Serafino, but he was reckoning without Don Franco's practical turn of mind.

"So far we've merely dealt with the rhetorical aspect," Don Franco protested. "We haven't even touched on what, if I may say so, is the heart of the matter. Don't you realize what a stroke of luck it is for an inconspicuous village like this to have been the birthplace of a man high up in politics?"

He opened a leather brief case and produced a folder bulging with documents and labeled PROJECTS. Everyone immediately understood what he had in mind.

"Do you really think it's a good idea," the mayor demanded, "to start pestering Andrea Cipriani with that kind of thing the moment he sets foot in the place? Wouldn't it be more intelligent to wait until the atmosphere's warmed up a bit?"

"We can't afford to waste time," the priest declared trenchantly. "We must strike while the iron's hot."

"Yes, I think we'd better move fast," the town clerk opined. "No one knows how long any party is going to stay in power." When one of the younger councilors frowned at the remark, he quickly added, "Alas."

Meanwhile Don Franco had opened his folder and was deploying his papers on the table.

"The dignity of Cisterna, not to mention its good name," he said, "requires first of all a monument to our fallen heroes, to be built at government expense. I hope you all agree that this should be our primary demand."

"One-third of our people are living in caves and shacks," protested the oldest councilor.

Don Franco had foreseen this objection and had his answer ready.

"Civilized people," he affirmed, "can be identified by the degree of importance they attach to the cult of the dead. Don't you think it's a disgrace that Cisterna should still be without a war memorial? Every one of us must find it painful."

"I haven't seen a monument like the one you're talking about in any of the other villages round here," the old councilor said.

"All the more reason for Cisterna to outshine them," Don Franco retorted in triumph. "Their envy will affirm our superiority."

"Quite a persuasive argument," the town clerk conceded with a titter.

"We're being asked to build a memorial to our fallen

31

heroes," one of the younger councilors put in. "All right, but which heroes? The heroes of the war of liberation?"

The mayor's jaw dropped, and he looked questioningly at Don Franco.

"I don't propose to let myself be drawn into controversy," the priest said curtly.

"But we can't build a monument to our dead heroes," the councilor insisted, "without specifying which ones."

"I did anticipate that difficulty," the priest admitted after a moment's embarrassment. "I've been thinking that, in order to get over it, it should be an allegorical monument. What would you say to a marble statue of Glory embracing Sacrifice?"

"What sacrifice?" the three councilors demanded simultaneously.

"The abstract idea of Sacrifice," Don Franco lashed back, red in the face. "The idea—the concept, that is. The idea includes everything."

But the principal objection was now put forward by the town clerk.

"Do you mean to say you'd let a thing like that be shown in a public place?" he asked, scandalized. "Bang in front of the parish church? Don Franco, I'm amazed at you. Where's your imagination? If the sculptor is to represent Glory embracing Sacrifice, he'll have to make a statue of a woman in the act of kissing a man. Didn't that occur to you? And what's more, it's not just a question of a movie; that kiss, in solid marble, will go on forever. Do you realize what that means? Day and night, rain or shine, without letting up for a minute, that woman will be kissing that man. A fine example, I must say, for the little girls in your catechism class."

"It'd be enough to turn any man's stomach, no matter how bent on sacrifice he was," the mayor commented with a grimace of disgust.

Red-faced, the priest hastened to propose some variations.

"We could have Glory stroking Sacrifice's head—a sort of maternal caress," he said. "Or would you rather she just smiled at him?"

The old councilor too was opposed to the scheme, but for a different reason. Glory, declared the old councilor, should take no interest whatsoever in Sacrifice, and should even refuse to look him in the face, until Sacrifice was ready to devote himself to the poor people still living in caves and shacks.

"My second project will be concerned with the welfare of the common people," said Don Franco, who was now in a slightly chastened mood; and to prove his words, he opened his brief case and extracted another folder.

"But how do you know we're not wasting our breath?" the old councilor broke in suddenly, rising to his feet. "What makes you take it for granted that Andrea Cipriani will agree to our proposals?"

These words, uttered in an almost defiant tone, fell like a cold shower on the priest's constructive fervor. He looked to right and left, waiting for the mayor to dispel the pessimistic mood and thus enable him to expound his other projects. But the mayor's brow was gloomy.

"Frankly, I don't know what to say," he admitted.

"We mustn't lose sight of the fact that Cipriani's been away from here nearly twelve years. He's been in prison; in a penal colony; he's fought as a partisan commander; and tomorrow he's coming back to Cisterna for the first time. How can we possibly guess what he's got up his sleeve?"

"Then why are we wasting our time?" Don Franco complained pettishly.

"We're waiting for Don Serafino," the mayor said. "He may know more than we do. I think he's been in correspondence with Cipriani."

"Good-by till tomorrow," said the parish priest, offended. He swept his papers together, rose to his feet and departed. The three councilors filed out after him, having suddenly realized that it was suppertime.

"Strictly in confidence," the town clerk asked the mayor, after glancing around to make sure that no one was listening, "strictly in confidence, could you tell me just where this Cipriani stands? Politically, I mean."

"As far as I can make out," the mayor replied, "he's what they call a humanitarian."

The town clerk almost choked with laughter.

"You're not serious?" he said. "Then, strictly in confidence, he's a complete imbecile."

"Complete," the mayor assured him.

CHAPTER FOUR

DON SERAFINO had barely returned home from early Mass when there was a knock at the door. His housekeeper went to investigate. At first she failed to recognize the tall lean young man on the doorstep. Standing there in shorts, open-necked shirt and beret, and covered from head to foot with the dust of a long ride, he had an air of authority. He had arrived on a motorcycle, which was leaning against the wall of the house, with a small valise strapped to the carrier behind the saddle.

"Who is it, please?" she inquired, holding the door half open. "And that's not the proper dress for a priest's house, young man."

"Andrea Cipriani," said the man with a smile.

The name brought Don Serafino hurrying; he was no less surprised than the old housekeeper.

"What a wonderful surprise," he exclaimed gaily. "We weren't expecting you till midday. Have you been to the town hall? Do come in. I suppose you've heard that the town council is in the hands of your friends."

"My friends?" Andrea laughed sardonically. "Before I

take a look at them I'd be curious to know just who they are. In fact, I got here early just in order to find out what varieties of torture you've been thinking up for me."

"And you mean to say you'd trust what I tell you?" the priest said in a tone of affectionate irony. "But sit down; we can talk while we're drinking our coffee. How many years have you actually been away? Let's count."

"I know you pretty well," said Andrea slowly, "and I'm bound to confess that on some points I wouldn't trust you completely. Politics, for instance. You've never been able to understand the first thing about them, and by instinct you're a rather narrow-minded conservative."

"Quite true," the priest agreed. "Thanks. As a matter of fact, in view of the times we live in, I'm rather inclined to accept your verdict as a compliment."

"But I also happen to know that you're straight as a die and totally loyal, and that you've never been an opportunist," Andrea added. "All of which—in view, as you say, of the times—are more or less unusual virtues."

"Sit down and stop flattering me," the priest told him. "Our coffee will be ready in a moment. As for today's ceremony in honor of your return, I need only say this much: the flag of local patriotism will be waving."

He pronounced these last words with a wry emphasis.

"I abhor patriotism in every form," Andrea said disgustedly. "I'm more interested in people. Tell me, who will be underfoot today?"

"That's what I was trying to explain," the priest said. "All Cisterna will be there. It's your native village, after all. You know all about it."

"Yes, but I've been away for so long."

"You needn't worry—it hasn't changed. There are a few scoundrels, and a few honest but stupid people. And for the rest—the usual majority of sheep and goats. And as if compulsory schooling weren't enough to turn these poor people into idiots, they've now got the movies and the radio into the bargain. Honestly, they were better off when they couldn't read or write. As for the poor, don't cherish any illusions about them. They're neither serious enough nor tough enough to make a revolution. But I can see you're not very pleased with my description. Well, you said it yourself a little while ago: I never did have much of a head for politics."

"Who's running the council now?" Andrea asked.

There was a pause before the priest replied.

"I'd rather not tell you what I think of them," he said finally, biting his lip. "I'd probably be unfair. The council needs your support; if I criticize anyone, I might be doing more harm than good. That Cisterna's in a pretty bad way you'll have already seen for yourself. Don't you care?"

Andrea grimaced.

"I see you're infected with local patriotism yourself," he said.

They broke off the conversation while the housekeeper served the coffee. The sallow, shrunken old spinster had tears in her eyes from the excitement of seeing Andrea again. She had forgotten, in her haste, to undo the two curling pins at her temples.

"Don Andrea," she kept repeating.

But Andrea protested.

"I'm not a priest," he said.

"And to think," she said, "that when you were little I often held you on my lap."

"I'll bet you wouldn't dare do it now, though," said Andrea, straight-faced.

"In my presence!" Don Serafino protested with mock severity. "Such scandalous carryings-on in my presence!"

The old servant, in a flurry of excitement, spilled some coffee on the guest's shorts. This sent her into paroxysms of confusion.

"No harm done," said Andrea, laughing. "They're filthy anyhow."

"You'd better change into something else for the reception," Don Serafino reminded him. "Tell me," he went on, "what are your plans?"

Andrea did not reply immediately. He was looking at the titles of the books on the shelves: Saint Justin, Saint Camillus of Lellis, Saint John of Capestrano, Saint Gabriel of Our Lady of Sorrows . . . The room was small, humble and stuffy.

"Is this where you spend your days?" he asked the priest. "How do you breathe?"

"I like staying in one place," Don Serafino told him. "I'm not a nomad. But we mustn't waste any more time. Before I go into what really needs to be done in Cisterna I'd like to tell you about one very sad individual case."

"You mean you're going to ask me to do a personal favor for someone?" Andrea interrupted.

"Yes, I am," the priest said. "I think you'll agree it's a genuinely deserving case."

"I'm sorry," Andrea said, "but I've promised myself not to get involved in personal questions. Tragic individual cases—I know they exist; but they should be handed over to the people specifically competent to deal with them—mayors, lawyers, doctors, midwives, priests. Please don't be offended. It's just that my idea of a politician seems to be different from the usual one. I think a politician ought to concentrate on the problems that affect the community as a whole, and not on doing favors for individuals."

Don Serafino smiled.

"Bravo," he said. "I congratulate you. But how long do you thing you're going to be able to abide by these excellent resolutions?"

"You shouldn't be the one to discourage me."

"I tell you, I admire you," Don Serafino continued, abruptly changing his tone to one of seriousness. "But if you only knew, my boy, what good intentions I had when I was ordained a priest."

"If I find I can't stick to my principles," said Andrea resolutely, "I'll give up politics."

"I'm sure you're quite capable of it," the priest hastened to declare. "So I won't insist. But before we leave this topic, I just want to say that I expressed myself rather clumsily a moment ago. I shouldn't have spoken in terms of personal favors. Not only did I crash headlong into your sacred principles—I also gave you an unfair impression of the man I want to tell you about. I can assure you he's not the kind of parasite that tries to get jobs or curry favor by exploiting his nuisance value or promising his vote at the next election. Far from it. Where pride and dignity are concerned, believe me, he's your equal. For the rest, how can I explain? It's not easy. He was born and bred here, yet even to me he's always been a puzzle. Indeed, I can say without exaggeration that nothing else in my life has ever puzzled me as much. . . . But now that we're talking of him, it suddenly comes back to me that from boyhood on he was your father's best friend. Ah, if only your father were alive today, we wouldn't need to go asking help from anyone else. Between us, we'd see to it that this man wasn't left destitute as he is now."

"What's his name?" Andrea asked.

"You couldn't have known him," the priest said. "In fact, nobody in Cisterna knows him, except half a dozen of the old folk. When were you born? Well, he was arrested a couple of years before that, and accused of highway robbery and murder. He was sent to prison on the strength of some scraps of evidence that seemed to point against him. I can't even begin to make you understand what that appalling trial meant to many of us. Everything about it was mysterious—most of all the attitude of the accused. He simply wouldn't defend himself. Then, just a few months ago—not far from here, in Perticara—another man confessed to the crime on his deathbed, and provided conclusive proof. So, after forty years, they set the innocent man free, and now he's back here, without one penny of compensation."

Andrea gave a start, and his face stiffened.

40

"You're not by any chance telling me about Luca Sabatini?" he asked.

"Yes, he's the very man. How did you guess his name?"

"You mean Luca's here? Can I see him? Don Serafino, I beg you, take me to him this instant. . . . It's true that I never knew him, but you'd be astonished if I told you all that Luca stands for in my life."

CHAPTER FIVE

"I CAN'T even offer you a chair," Luca apologized.

Andrea smiled.

"I'm not tired," he said.

Luca dragged over a big rock for his guest to sit on. The ant heap beneath scattered in all directions.

"We'll find you more comfortable quarters," Andrea reassured him.

"There's no hurry," Luca answered. "As long as the fine weather lasts I can manage quite nicely here."

A lantern dangled from a beam by a piece of wire. Half a loaf, an onion and two tomatoes had been set out on the wooden crate that did duty for a table. The bed was a large sack, stuffed with straw and laid on the bare flagstones. Luca fetched a bottle of wine and a cup from a recess in the wall and filled the cup for his guest. As he poured his hand trembled.

"At least here's something to drink," he said. "I wonder if you know how good it tastes, when one's just out of prison—that first glass of wine from the vineyards of one's

42

childhood? And how wonderful it feels to be able to light a fire again with one's own hands."

His eyes glistened.

"What a horror it must have been," Andrea said, "for a man like you, so alive, to eat prison bread for a whole lifetime."

"Well, it's past remedy now." Luca smiled at him. "Anyway, you've had a fairly rough time of it yourself. Don't be surprised, Andrea, but I know a good deal about you. A man from Celano told me about you, a fellow prisoner at Civitavecchia. I've been expecting you ever since."

"Where? In prison?"

"Yes, I'd got it into my head that you were born branded, like me."

"Branded? Well, perhaps you're right," Andrea said. "But I wasn't born that way. I'd say it was life that branded me—rather prematurely. Mind, Luca"—Andrea's voice was suddenly grave—"this is a story that concerns you."

"Me?" exclaimed Luca.

Andrea hesitated.

"When Don Serafino mentioned you a little while ago," he said firmly, "the news took me completely by surprise; yet now that I've met you, I can see that I've been waiting all my life for this meeting. You see I've been carrying this story around inside me ever since I was a child, and you're the only one who could possibly understand it."

"Did your father tell you about me?" Luca asked. "Did you know that he and I were great friends?"

"Not only my father," said Andrea. "A lot of people in

Cisterna still talked about you when I was a boy. Even though many years had gone by and there had been other bloody crimes—whenever people spoke of the Trial they invariably meant yours. That sort of conversation was broken off of course when children were around. But Teresa, your mother, talked to me about you very often. It was all she had to live for, poor old woman—her memories of you. She was a Mater Dolorosa whose son had been taken from her. Her life stopped short, you might say, the day you were sentenced."

At these words Luca's eyes misted with tears.

"In her very first letters," he said, "she told me she was helping in your household."

"Not as a servant, though," Andrea explained. "In spite of all her misfortunes she still kept her pride. My father never thought of her except as the mother of his best friend. Let me think back a little and try to remember."

"Sit down and talk to me about her," Luca said. "Tell me, did she ever sing? When I lived at home she was always singing—when she was washing clothes, kneading dough."

"Yes, at evening she used to sing my baby brother to sleep," said Andrea. "Such sweet, sad lullabies they were. She may have made them up herself. My mother used to say she'd never heard any like them."

Luca hid his face in his hands.

"Forgive me," he said. "Pay no attention. I know you were only a child at the time, but whatever else you can remember about her, no matter if it's sad, please tell me. Not that I believe tears can fill up forty years of emptiness."

44

"I was eight or nine years old, in third grade, when your mother got your first letter."

"I had just come out of solitary confinement," Luca explained. "It was like being buried alive. Up to then I wasn't allowed to write."

"Your mother was an intelligent woman, as you know, well above the average for women of her background, but she'd never gone to school and she couldn't read or write."

"Yes, that was common enough in those days. Teaching women to read and write was still considered a waste, if not a sin. The important thing, for a woman like her, was to know her prayers—and you didn't have to read prayers, you learned them by heart."

"I became very fond of your mother," Andrea went on. "My parents did everything to encourage it. I spent most of my free time with her. My father used to call us 'the sweethearts.' I remember the time she got your first letter as clearly as though it were today. It was evening. I was alone in the kitchen when your mother returned from the fountain with a brimming pitcher balanced on her head. She set it down in its corner. Then, out of that stiff bodice they used to wear in those days, she drew a letter. In a very low voice she asked me if I would read her what you had written and write down her reply. It was a proof of her trust, and I was filled with pride at such an honor. But I mustn't breathe a word about it to anyone, she warned me, not even to my parents. She didn't like to let other people know about her troubles, she explained, except me, because I was still an innocent. I agreed then and there. Your mother can scarcely have realized the gravity of

45

what she was asking, and I had no means of guessing
how profound an effect that correspondence would have on
me. I hope you'll forgive me, Luca, if I tell you now that
it was one of the most important events in my life. In
fact—and I'm not exaggerating—it may even have been
the crucial one. It cut short my childhood; it was my introduction to human suffering. I was at an age, you must remember, when reading and writing are still very difficult,
and then there was the additional strain of secrecy. I had
to make innumerable drafts of every letter, and innumerable copies of the final draft, before it could be mailed.
Your mother would dictate to me in a low, cautious tone
—did she always have that hushed voice? She didn't speak
—she whispered. She would murmur a sentence, ponder
over it, then straightaway correct it. In her loneliness she
talked to me as though I were a grown person, using
words that I could only guess at, and making incomprehensible allusions. I used to despair of understanding her.
Those words, those sighs were for me the portent of a
world as yet unknown. I was terrified, but I tried to hide
it. Your mother talked to me without realizing the profound reverberations of what she said. It wasn't that she'd
forgotten that I was little more than a baby; it was just
that she needed to communicate with someone. A person
that distressed will talk to his dog, or to a plant. When
she wept, as she often did, she would cram her handkerchief into her mouth to stifle her sobs. At first, to be frank
with you, I found it rather strange that a person as
thoughtful and conscientious as your mother should have
chosen me for so weighty a task, without my parents'

knowledge. One day I let her see my uneasiness. 'Do you believe that Luca's innocent?' Teresa asked me. 'Of course I do,' I said. 'Well,' she told me, 'the others all think he's guilty—guilty of that murder or maybe a different one, but guilty anyhow. That's why I won't turn to them.' "

"Did you really believe I was innocent? How? Why?" Luca asked.

"I was certain of it," Andrea answered. "But how or why, I can't possibly explain. Your mother had a way of affirming your innocence that simply left no room for doubt. Only very rarely, in later life, have I known that same sense of absolute certainty. I'd describe it now, in retrospect, as my first true, deeply felt experience of the communion of two souls. But my certainty led me straight to a big problem. 'If Luca didn't do anything bad,' I asked Teresa, 'why did they convict him?' 'It was his fate,' she told me. 'He couldn't escape it.' That word 'fate' gave injustice a terrifying weight, as if it were part of the natural order. Since it was inconceivable that my mother, or my teacher at school, or the parish priest could be wicked or deceitful, I began to think that injustice must in no sense depend on people's good or wicked nature. Cruelty must be just like bad weather. But then where was the dishonor in going to prison? Was honor, too, determined by fate? My brain reeled with all these painful, muddled attempts to understand. Small as I was, I already had a glimmering of what was to come. All this was a kind of premonition. So I felt no surprise when, years later, certain things happened to me. I'd been expecting them to happen. Life was like that. But it's hopeless—nothing I

say can really give you any idea of my confusion. Now
that I look back on that strange situation with a certain
amount of detachment, I'm inclined to think that your
mother may have had other reasons for entrusting her
replies to your letters to a child rather than an adult.
What I mean is, an older person would probably have
understood some of the remarks and the news she dictated
to me, whereas they were completely over my head. However, I had no such suspicion then; and in fact before long
I came to accept your mother's choice, with all the terror
and turmoil it was causing me, as evidence that fate had
singled me out. I guarded the secret scrupulously. I felt
that it contained the key to some dreadful mystery, some
aspect of life remote from anything I'd ever imagined,
and that my possession of it set me above my companions.
After all, I was no mere scribe. I was involved in a real
conspiracy, with a convict, and the mother of a convict.
Even now, Luca, I could quote from memory long pas-
sages from that correspondence of ours."

"The childish handwriting—how well I remember it,"
said Luca. "But of course I never imagined all this. I
remember, too, the way whole sentences were censored."

"You once asked your mother who was doing the writing
for her. Now that I think of it, I suppose you wanted to
make sure she wasn't being indiscreet."

"I got no answer though."

Andrea smiled.

"We had our secrets too, you know. Oh, I've still got
so much to tell you. I'd never been away from home, you
see, and I'd had no occasion to write any letters. So the

letters addressed to a convict were the first I ever wrote. My heart used to pound furiously all the time I was writing them down and copying them. I soon found myself avoiding the company of other boys. The river bank where we played our childish games already seemed remote, like some land I was leaving far behind. It was the innocent land where a Good Fairy brings gifts at Epiphany and mothers find their babies under rosebushes. I even began to neglect my lessons. They seemed futile compared to my secret task. A single letter would keep me busy for days on end. The monthly letter to you wasn't the only one—there were others to be written on your behalf. It wasn't easy for a boy in third grade to find the right expression for everything your mother would tell me, in dialect, about herself, her debts, the petitions to be addressed to the King, the Queen Mother, the Duke of Abruzzi, the Pope, and the daughter of General Garibaldi. The poor woman believed in fate, as I've told you, but she didn't rule out the possibility of Grace coming either from God or from the mighty of this world. What she didn't believe in for one moment—simply didn't waste her breath on—was justice. There were days when we spent all our free time in secret conclave. We generally met in your house because there was less likelihood of being disturbed. Naturally, my services were indispensable for the letters to the authorities. At the bottom of the page I had painstakingly prepared, your mother would sign with a cross. I already knew that people who couldn't read or write signed that way; but in any case, what could have been a more appropriate signature for your mother? A little cross—it suited her exactly.

I remember Don Serafino asking me at the catechism examination, the following year, to explain the sign of the cross. 'It reminds us of the Passion of Our Lord,' I told him, 'and it's also the way unfortunates sign their names.' The parish priest remarked that my answer wasn't wrong, but that I was hardly in a position to revise the answers in the catechism. Another thing that left a deep impression on me, when Don Serafino explained it to us in those same catechism lessons, was the word 'Revelation.' It used to cost me a terrific effort not to shout, at the top of my voice, Teresa's revelation about the world's injustice. . . . But perhaps I'm boring you," said Andrea. "What are these childish fancies, compared to your predicament?"

"I implore you to go on," Luca said with emotion. "Everything you've told me so far is tremendously important to me. Believe me."

"I don't know whether it can really be of any importance to you," said Andrea. "For me it's as though, in talking to you, I'd at last begun to understand my own life. As a child I was easily frightened, haunted by ridiculous fears. I'm telling you this now so that you won't imagine I hold your mother in any way to blame. On the contrary, the older I grow, the more grateful I am to her. Thanks to her, I became aware of the false front in human life. That's how I developed this mania of mine—this obsession, rather—for finding out what's behind it. Mind you, in some of these reminiscences I'm not sure of the exact borderline between what did in fact happen to me and what I only feared or hoped might happen. The secret magnified everything in proportion to what it hid. I soon began to

50

feel myself cut off from the everyday life around me. I grew moodier and more solitary. Strange ideas disturbed my mind. And I came to know the sorrow of the harshest solitude, the sorrow of being unable to confide to those I loved the reason for my inward agony. No one in my family—neither my mother nor my father nor my elder brother—had the faintest suspicion of what was going on. Their attempts to make me laugh nearly always produced the opposite result—I would be offended and burst into tears. My own sporadic efforts to be sociable failed just as dismally. One morning at the breakfast table, for instance, I told them that I'd slept badly and that, when I got up, my wrists were sore. 'They feel,' I said, 'just as though I'd been wearing handcuffs for hours and hours.' Coming from me, the remark must have sounded very funny, but it was a long time before I could forgive my family for the burst of laughter with which they greeted it, and which of course was echoed as the story went the rounds of friends and relatives. What was so amusing about it? Did they think I wasn't worthy of wearing handcuffs? Another time I was whiling away the afternoon alone in my little room, lying on the bed, when all at once I saw my mother standing in the doorway. I hadn't heard her footsteps, and I was startled. 'What do you want here, what are you looking for, why do you have to spy on me?' I shouted. My mother was understandably thunderstruck. She was carrying a little present for me; she'd come to give it to me. 'What's happening to you?' she asked. 'Don't you love me any more? Don't you trust me any more?' But what had trust and love got to do with it when trust and love didn't prevent innocent people from going to prison. Finally I fell sick. One evening I began to shiver violently, and during the night I developed a high fever. The doctor diagnosed pneumonia. It was a long illness. I had to stay in bed all winter, and I missed a whole school year. My mother and yours took turns sitting by my bedside. The moment I was rid of the fever I began writing to you again. But then, in the spring, it was your letters that stopped coming all of a sudden."

"That was because of what they called an act of insubordination on my part against the governor of the prison," said Luca. "They punished me for it with another year of solitary confinement."

"That was the year your mother died," Andrea said.

"Don Serafino wrote to tell me."

"There was such strength in her," Andrea went on, "and yet she was frail. Once or twice, while I was reading her your first letters, to my terror and bewilderment she fainted away. After that she always kept a little phial of vinegar by her, and at the first wave of faintness she'd hold it to her nostrils. Because of this, the smell of vinegar came to represent persecuted innocence in my mind. It was in that same vinegar, I used to think, that Pilate's legionaries soaked the sponge they held to the lips of Christ crucified when He complained of thirst."

Luca in the meanwhile had turned his back and begun to strip the green husks from some ears of corn; but at these words he stopped.

"When I think what your life has been . . ." Andrea left the sentence unfinished. Weary and thoughtful, he sat staring at the ground.

Luca came over and touched his shoulder.

"They're waiting for you at the town hall," he said. "It's time. The citizenry will all be there. There'll be speeches and refreshments."

Andrea, still in a kind of trance, gave no sign of having heard.

Finally he said: "Would you do one thing for me?"

"Of course," replied Luca. "Need you ask?"

"I assure you it's not idle curiosity on my part. It's just that I feel such a need to understand."

"What is it?"

"It was all so long ago," Andrea went on. "So many disasters have happened since then—an earthquake, three wars. There's hardly anyone left alive who remembers—you know that. You yourself, here among these ruins—it's as though you'd come back from the grave. If you look around you . . ."

He broke off, and there was another silence.

"You were going to ask me something," Luca reminded him.

"Why didn't you defend yourself at the trial?" Andrea burst out. "Why did you refuse to tell where you spent the night of the murder?"

Luca rose to his feet.

"I'm sorry," he said: "Believe me, Andrea, I'm truly sorry, especially after everything you've just told me. But I beg you not to insist on an answer to that question."

Andrea smiled.

"I won't insist," he said. "In fact, I withdraw it."

Tears welled up in Luca's eyes. He flung his arms open and drew Andrea into a long affectionate embrace.

Toni poked his head around the half-open door.

"So you're still here!" he exclaimed to Andrea. "I suppose you know they're all waiting for you at the town hall?"

"Don't breathe a word to anyone," Andrea said. "Here's money—go and buy us something to eat."

"Toni, don't go," Luca warned him. Then, to Andrea, he added: "You're my guest. I'm doing the providing. I'm going to boil this corn right away."

CHAPTER SIX

"You've gone too far this time," Don Serafino exclaimed in a tone of mock outrage. "Where, may I ask, did you acquire such manners? You kept mayor, corporation, parish priest and police all standing around waiting for you till two o'clock. Do you realize how ridiculous you've made them look in front of the entire village?"

"Didn't you wait for me too?" Andrea asked. "I'd be disappointed if you hadn't."

"Of course I did," Don Serafino told him. "But I was the only one to guess that you wouldn't come, the only one to know the real reason for your not coming—and further-more," he added, his eyes beginning to twinkle, "the only one able to enjoy the whole performance secretly."

"I hope you didn't tell them where I was or with whom."

"No, I play-acted beautifully. It was great fun. I roused my neighbors against you. 'It's downright scandal-ous,' I kept telling them. 'It's a bad beginning for the new regime. If I were the mayor I'd resign this minute.' The most disgruntled of the lot, to give him his due, was Don Franco. He'd been lying in wait for you with a whole battery of scrolls under his arm. From the moment he arrived, he never stopped telling us how all the nearby villages would be dying of envy. That's really his religious ideal—building-projects *ad infinitum*. So you can imagine how disappointed he was. Finally, when it got to be very late, the mayor went out on the balcony and announced, for the benefit of the few people still waiting outside the town hall, that you'd been delayed by some minor accident. This was received with hoots of laughter. You must have been recognized when you left my house this morning. Nevertheless I'm forced to admit that on the whole I approve of you, Andrea. Let's put it this way: you're better than I expected."

"You seem to be amused by scandals."

"Well, yes, and if they happen to discredit the secular powers, they really cheer me up. Now all I have to do is find out what happened to those cakes and bottles of vermouth bought at public expense for your reception."

Don Serafino's study was a low-ceilinged, dark-paneled room, dimly lit by two tiny windows.

"It's like a bat's cave," Andrea said.

"I call that an unmannerly remark," the priest told him.

The walls were partly hidden by shelves of dusty books and files. A small plaster statue of the Good Shepherd stood under a glass dome on the chimney piece. The air smelled vaguely of mildew. Don Serafino, crouched over a little oilcloth-covered table with a pile of exercise books in front of him and a huge red pencil in his hand, was correcting the work of the private pupils whom he tutored in Latin. He looked very old as he sat there, drawing one difficult breath after another through his half-open lips.

56

The skull was doing duty as a paperweight. Beside the window that gave onto the garden, Andrea looked at the morning papers and smoked his pipe. The doorbell rang insistently. Don Serafino went to open it and stayed talking for a while with the people gathered outside.

"It's you they're asking for," he told Andrea. "Why not have them in here one at a time?"

"Who are they and what do they want?"

"They're just poor people, that's all. One of them wants a pension; others want unemployment relief."

"Why don't they go to the mayor?"

"It was the mayor himself who sent them to you. You ought to hear what they have to say," Don Serafino added. "I can vouch for them—they really are destitute."

"And if I were to help them to get what they want, their lives would be transformed?" Andrea exploded. "Well, that's not the kind of help I want them to ask me for."

Don Serafino went back to the door and said a few words. Then he returned to his table and began correcting another Latin exercise.

"By the way," he remarked, turning toward Andrea, "I forgot to tell you that among the victims of your rudeness yesterday there were a few innocent ones."

"Who, for instance?"

"Your dear old Aunt Clarice."

"Poor aunt. What did she want of me?"

"It seems she'd prepared a banquet in your honor."

"That's the first I've heard of it. If she'd told me, I'd have talked her out of it."

"You had to eat somewhere," Don Serafino protested.

"As a matter of fact, it was I who made the suggestion, to get you out of having to accept an invitation from the mayor. I said you might prefer to be with your relatives. Anyhow, she's expecting you tonight. I promised her you wouldn't fail to turn up this time."

"A nice mess you've got me into," Andrea said grumpily. "What's Luca doing now?"

"He's upstairs in his room—taking a nap, I expect, or else sitting at his window and looking at the countryside."

"I'll write a note to Aunt Clarice begging off. May I ask your housekeeper to deliver it?"

"My housekeeper has left," the priest said. "Didn't I tell you? No sooner had Luca moved in than the old harridan flung her apron on the floor and quit, without even giving me a week's notice. Luca doesn't know, of course."

"Even your housekeeper . . . What on earth could she have against him?"

"Presumably the fact that he's spent his life in prison."

"Doesn't she realize he was innocent?"

"Yes, of course she does. So do they all. And yet . . ."

Into Andrea's face there came a look of mingled exasperation and despondency.

"Christ, what people!" he said. "They've been through one cataclysm after another, and they're still exactly the same."

"We'll manage to make our beds somehow," Don Serafino went on. "That shouldn't be too difficult. But for the rest, it's a bother, at my age, to have to do without a servant."

58

"With so much poverty in the neighborhood," said Andrea, "surely it won't take you long to find a new one, even if she's not perfect."

"So you may think; but Canon Law forbids me to employ a young woman—she's got to be at least forty," the priest explained. "And none of the older ones will set foot in this house now, I can assure you, no matter how badly they may need the money, for the same reason that this one had for leaving."

"In short, they all seem to be afraid of Luca," Andrea burst out. "But why?"

Don Serafino's face clouded, and he was silent for a while.

"When I first heard that Luca was coming back, I must confess that I was frightened too," he said finally. "Don't ask me why—I can't understand it myself. I even went so far as to suggest—indirectly, through the sergeant—that arrangements might be made for Luca to settle down in some hospice or other, a long way off."

Andrea swung round to face the priest.

"You! What could you possibly have been afraid of?" he demanded, looking him straight in the eyes.

"I was his parish priest," Don Serafino answered in an evasive tone. "A parish priest is responsible for his parishioners."

"I know, but that's no reason for being afraid," Andrea persisted. "I can't make you out."

From the mounting embarrassment Don Serafino's face betrayed under the assault of Andrea's questions, it looked as though the discussion had caught him off guard.

"Listen, Andrea"—the old priest's tone was half pleading, half apologetic—"these are things you can't understand, if you'll forgive me for saying so. You weren't even born when they happened."

"But in those few years," Andrea cried, "human nature didn't change."

"I beg you not to raise your voice," Don Serafino said. "Luca might hear us. Take my word for it," he added, "even if you knew all there is to know, you'd still find yourself up against a mystery."

Andrea gave a scornful laugh.

"That word is a bit too convenient," he said. "You priests invariably trot it out whenever you want to escape from a tight corner."

"I didn't think you could be so coarse," the priest exclaimed. "Don't forget it's Luca we're talking about, not me. Here's one point you might think about—if you're able to. Luca was tremendously moved by his meeting with you, but in spite of that, he refused to give the explanation you asked for. Don't you think his privacy deserves to be respected?"

"Of course," Andrea admitted. "You're quite right. But I assure you it isn't idle curiosity that makes me want to find out. How can I explain? Well, the fact is, Luca's secret concerns me too."

"It seems to concern everybody, in one way or another," Don Serafino observed testily.

He was standing now, looking out at the street through a small window protected by two crossed bars. The failing light shone on his snowy hair and painted greenish shadows

60

on his white face. After a pause he went on: "I don't know if I told you . . ."

"You've told me nothing at all," Andrea interrupted.

"But what do you expect me to tell you?" Don Serafino asked, as if stung. "You're not my confessor. I was merely going to say, before you leave . . ."

"I don't intend leaving for the present," Andrea retorted harshly. "Have you any objection?"

"Please don't be insolent," the priest said. "Why on earth should I object?"

There was a painful silence. Andrea picked up his newspapers again, while Don Serafino stood with his back to Andrea, his face against the iron bars of the window.

"Here comes a visitor for you," he announced presently, without turning round. "Your Aunt Clarice."

Andrea sprang to open the door himself. The lady he found waiting on the doorstep, although no longer young, was still slender and graceful, and her black dress had a certain old-fashioned elegance.

"Dear Aunt Clarice," said Andrea, "it seems you were expecting me for lunch yesterday. I'm truly sorry to have upset your arrangements, but I heard nothing about it until a few minutes ago."

"Yes, there was some misunderstanding; it was a great pity," said the lady. "We waited for you till two o'clock."

"Won't you come in for a moment? Don Serafino will be cross with me . . ."

"Don Serafino has seen plenty of me already, both yesterday and today, all because of you. Andrea, I hope we may count on you for dinner this evening, at least. It's been so many years since we've laid eyes on you."

"I'm off again this evening, I'm afraid," Andrea told her. "I'm kept rather busy at present, you know. And there's a friend I've got to meet again before I leave."

"Why don't you bring him along too? Or aren't we good enough?"

"Of course you are—but won't it be a bother?"

"On the contrary, it will be an honor, if he's a friend of yours. Who is he? A foreigner? Somebody important?"

"No, he comes from here. He used to be a great friend of my father's. I don't know if the name means anything to you—Luca Sabatini."

"The convict?"

"The ex-convict, to be precise."

"You mean you'd bring an ex-convict into my house?" Aunt Clarice exclaimed. Her gentle eyes, round as cherries, filled with horror.

"Aunt Clarice," pleaded Andrea, "you may not be aware of it, but the poor man was innocent."

"Innocent or not, he was a convict. Andrea, how could you think of introducing such an individual . . ."

"Aunt Clarice, please don't talk like that. I thought I told you he was a friend of mine."

"Of course, Andrea, I fully realize, you're in politics now, and you're not free to pick and choose your acquaintances. All the same, I do think you might be a little reasonable. A private house is a different matter, and I've got two marriageable daughters. Fiorella, the elder, is on the point of becoming engaged. . . ."

"Aunt Clarice, I assure you that my friendship with

62

Luca has nothing whatsoever to do with politics. It's just that, quite frankly, in all Cisterna he's the person I value most."

"Poor, poor Andrea!" exclaimed Aunt Clarice. She was so overwhelmed that she could say no more; to escape her embarrassment, she fled, scurrying off without even saying good-by.

Her daughters had been standing behind the wrought-iron grille of a ground-floor window, watching for her return. They were greatly alarmed to see her looking so upset.

"What happened?" asked Fiorella. "Are you not feeling well, Mamma?"

"Oh, my darlings," Signora Clarice murmured, in a voice that trembled on the verge of sobbing, "your cousin is mad, stark, staring mad."

CHAPTER SEVEN

THE old judge had retired long ago, but he had kept the brass plate on the door of his villa, and he still had within reach on his desk the volumes and yellowing back numbers of the *Official Gazette*. At the name of Andrea Cipriani, he looked up at his visitor, then dropped his eyes to the letter of introduction, then stared again at the man standing in front of him, and then, leaning heavily on a stick, got up from his armchair.

"Signor Cipriani? The schoolmaster? H'm, er, delighted to see you. Carolina!" he shouted. "Carolina! Coffee! Yes, yes, I was expecting you, Signor Cipriani. I've heard you spoken of by the presiding judge of the Court of Appeal. Very favorably. H'm. Very favorably indeed, as a matter of fact. Times have changed, of course. . . ."

The old judge, limping slightly, took Andrea by the arm and led him down a dark narrow passage to the drawing room.

"Shall we sit on the divan? I think we'll find the little table here useful. You see this pile of mildewed documents, Signor Cipriani? Take a look at the label."

64

"You mean these are the actual court records of the Sabatini case?" Andrea was unable to repress his excitement. "Before coming to Aquila I was afraid they'd been destroyed."

"Here they are, by special permission," the old judge explained in his squeaky voice. "I needed to consult them— I'm writing my reminiscences, you know. What did you say? Are they finished? Not yet, but they're coming on nicely. That's how I spend my days now—remembering the past. Memory is my refuge. Thanks to it, today's world seems far away, which is all that makes it endurable. That's why I seldom go out and then only after dark. I say this with all due respect to you, since from what I'm told you're a man of today."

"In fact, of tomorrow," Andrea corrected him with a grin.

"Worse still," the old judge declared ponderously. "Much worse. Ah, well, we're on the downgrade now. How we're ever going to climb back again I cannot think. Please take a seat. Do you smoke?"

Andrea was eager to come to the point.

"I understand," he said, "that you were the public prosecutor at Luca Sabatini's trial?"

"Yes indeed, and upon my word I'm still proud of the way I conducted that case. People now have simply no conception of what a summing-up could be like in the old days."

"But even then, brilliant oratory was no guarantee against judicial error," Andrea objected. "*Errare humanum est*—we have to resign ourselves to that."

"I don't quite catch the drift of your argument."

"Well, I expect you heard that Luca Sabatini's innocence was finally established a few months ago."

"Fiddlesticks!" exclaimed the old judge, giving the floor a whack with his cane. "No disrespect intended to you, of course. But may I point out that Sabatini wasn't exonerated: he was pardoned. There's quite a difference, you know—quite a difference."

"In this case it's a purely formal difference," observed Andrea.

"But allow me to remind you, my dear sir, that form is everything, in the law just as in art." He paused, and then repeated: "Just as in art."

"A pardon," said Andrea patiently, "was not only the quickest way out, but also the cheapest. To exonerate him, as you know better than I do, would have entailed a fresh trial—lawyers, documents, the whole devilish bag of tricks. But Sabatini has neither money nor relatives, and he's beyond caring for legal forms."

"No, no, no!" the old judge reiterated vehemently. "You can't explain things away in such a childish fashion. The state provides legal aid free of charge for the indigent. I'm sorry, did you say you smoked?"

"Not now, thank you."

The old judge lit a cigarette and inserted it in a long black holder. Behind the urbane manner and the brittle fragility, there seemed to lurk a rather ambiguous little person. With his yellow face and lack-luster eyes, he vaguely resembled an owl. His few remaining hairs had all too obviously been dyed—black, with a coffee-colored tinge—and were plastered in thin streaks across the shining dome of his head. Andrea glanced around him. He felt uncomfortable. Faded though they were, the heavy purple curtains gave the room the shadowy half light of some questionable boudoir. A massive volume lay open on a tall lectern by one of the windows; above the lectern hung a wire cage with two canaries, both of them asleep. On the wall over the old judge's head King Umberto I and Queen Margherita looked down from an enormous framed photograph.

"Mind you, Signor Cipriani," he went on, "personally I've got no objection whatsoever to Sabatini's pardon. Why should I? What do I care about him one way or the other? But if he were to ask for the case to be reopened, and if I—this is pure hypothesis, of course—were again to act as public prosecutor, well, I can assure you, Signor Cipriani, that I would demand the confirmation, pure and simple, of the original sentence. And what's more, let me tell you, I'd get it."

"You don't seem to have heard what happened a few months ago," said Andrea doggedly. "A man in Perticara confessed to that murder on his deathbed, and cleared Sabatini of all connection with it."

"I know everything," the old judge assured him. He paused significantly. "Everything," he repeated. "Thanks to the courtesy of a colleague of the Law Courts, I was given access to a verbatim transcript of that man's statement. I studied it quite carefully, as a matter of fact; the episode having been of some importance to my career in the law. Well, Signor Cipriani, his statement failed to convince me."

"How can you possibly say such a thing?" Andrea protested in amazement. "Not only did the man confess his guilt—he gave proofs. I presume you know that his information led to their finding the victim's watch and wallet in a bricked-up hiding place. Isn't that enough?"

The old man's sallow face disintegrated into an ironic laugh.

"No, my dear sir, it's not enough," he said. "Not enough to justify what you are claiming. The new evidence doesn't invalidate the evidence on which Sabatini was convicted. At most it can be said to lend weight to the suspicion— clearly formulated in my summing-up—that he had accomplices."

"Well, I'm convinced of the reverse," Andrea declared emphatically. "I've got no doubts whatsoever. I find that . . ."

"May I tell you something, Signor Cipriani?" the old judge broke in. "May I? Your convictions are a matter of supreme indifference to me."

He waved his hand vaguely, in what was perhaps intended to be a gesture of polite dismissal; but Andrea was poring over the documents and completely failed to notice it. The old judge sat with his cane between his knees, clasping the ivory knob in his little yellow hands. He had lapsed again into the air of boredom and apathy that made him look like an owl, but every now and then he half opened his eyelids, as if to keep watch on the movements of his guest.

"Might I have a look at these documents?" Andrea asked him abruptly.

"They're entirely at your disposal," the old judge replied. "I've finished with them myself, and I'm officially authorized to pass them on to you before I return them to the archives. They won't make light reading, I warn you, but at least I think you'll find them pretty straightforward. It was the jury, when all's said and done, that decided the outcome of the trial; and the jurors were all decent honest men, farmers and shopkeepers for the most part. By the time you get to the end, I think you'll see why they returned a verdict of guilty."

"Judicial errors can be made in good faith," said Andrea.

"Read the documents, Signor Cipriani," the old judge insisted peevishly. "They will convince you of Sabatini's guilt, despite your preconceived ideas. I think I can safely say that you'll find it confirmed on every page; but should you feel inclined to skip, I suggest you read at least the eyewitness accounts of his behavior the evening before the fatal hold-up. He announced his intention of committing the crime, in unmistakable terms, and in his fiancée's very home. Then there was his behavior during the investigation and the public hearing. And finally . . ."

"I understand," said Andrea. "You're alluding to the fact that Luca Sabatini refused to explain where and with whom he spent the night of the murder. As far as I'm concerned, knowing nothing about the reasons for his stubborn silence, it seems perfectly conceivable that a man should keep silent for reasons of honor, at whatever cost to himself."

"Ah, no, my dear sir, your romantic notions have led you astray this time," the old judge exclaimed with open scorn. "You'd like to attribute such chivalrous ideals to a clodhopper like him! My word, you make me laugh! You'd put a fine leather saddle on a pack mule. Well, you certainly have imagination. A common peasant capable of choosing life imprisonment rather than reveal a secret? A common peasant with the code of a feudal knight? Very likely, I must say."

His sarcasm had literally transformed the old judge from an owl to a hawk.

"A peasant may be capable of suffering in ways that a judge can't even conceive of," Andrea retorted, not at all cowed.

"Please don't talk nonsense, Signor Cipriani. Were you born in a rural area? One would never guess it. You know as well as I do: a peasant's capacity for suffering is entirely physical; he can feel hunger and he can feel it when he's beaten. But the pangs of love! Holy Virgin! The tragic passion that, in the beloved's absence, feeds on dreams of her! It simply doesn't exist for the peasant, any more than it does for the middle class. It was a privilege reserved to the aristocracy. When there still was an aristocracy," he added after a pause.

A telephone rang in the passage, and a strident female voice could be heard answering it. The old judge twisted his head round toward the hall and shouted: "Tell them to call back later." Then he went on: "Believe me, Signor Cipriani, an innocent man would never accept the dreadful penalty of imprisonment without first telling everything he knows and, furthermore, inventing whatever might serve his cause. There are only two examples known to history of innocent men remaining silent before a judge—Jesus and Socrates. Now I don't suppose you'll go so far as to exalt this criminal from your village . . ."

The way he pronounced the word "criminal" angered Andrea.

"Why are you so down on the poor man?" he cried.

"He's a chapter in my autobiography," the old judge answered blandly. "And that particular chapter, I might as well tell you, I am ready to defend tooth and nail."

These last words rang with a note of genuine sincerity that had previously been absent in his voice.

"And now," he pursued, "forgive me if I in turn ask you a question: why are you so interested in this fellow?"

"I don't altogether understand what you mean," Andrea said.

"This Luca Sabatini—is he by any chance a relative?"

"No, he's a friend. My best friend, actually."

"Oh," said the old judge. For a moment he remained comically open-mouthed. "I beg your pardon," he said. "I beg your pardon." Then, recovering his composure, he went on: "And is this—er—friendship of long standing?"

"Thirty years or so."

"Thirty years? I don't quite follow. . . . He was in prison then. How could you possibly . . .?"

Andrea shrugged, as if to say that it would take too long to explain. "You see," he said in a conciliatory tone, "I'd like to leave friendship out of it and be objective. Luca seems to me an ordinary man, a peasant like so many others, except for being more unfortunate. What was exceptional was the circumstances he found himself face

71

to face with. And it seems to me that he dealt with them in a most unordinary way."

"And now, with all due respect to your friendship, may I too speak freely?" the old judge asked. "You don't mind? Well, personally I don't believe that an ordinary individual can ever become a superman by force of circumstance. He may try to bluff; he may pose as a superman. But his bluff won't stand up to an ordeal as prolonged and hideous as life imprisonment. You know, Signor Cipriani, how badly our pseudo-supermen have ended. And for heaven's sake let's not talk of supermen when it comes to relations with women. There's no such thing as a superman in underpants, you can take it from me."

The old judge spoke as if he were dictating to his clerk. Visibly pleased by his talent for improvisation, he settled himself more comfortably on the divan, joined his palms and continued: "You know as well as I do that in this country, whenever a man has an amorous adventure, he can hardly wait to make a good story out of it. I don't know about other countries; to an Italian his adventure would lose all its charm without the admiration and envy of his friends. Adultery without jealousy would disgust even a traveling salesman. In Italy we seek out such adventures chiefly in order to boast about them. Let's face it, Signor Cipriani—where would the fun be otherwise? The conquest of a woman sets a public seal on our virility. Tell me, now: without the publicity, would it really be worth the trouble? What would it amount to? It would either be depravity or plain gymnastics."

"Your honor's aphorisms are witty, but too general,"

said Andrea with distaste. "Unfortunately I've got no concrete arguments to oppose them with, because Sabatini told me nothing and I haven't yet seen the records."

"Well, read the records and you'll be forced to admit that I'm right," said the old judge with finality. "I'm convinced that Luca Sabatini remained silent and didn't invent an alibi through sheer lack of imagination. Through simple stupidity."

"He doesn't strike one as being stupid," Andrea broke in.

"He's a primitive, and a violent one, this—h'm—friend of yours, if you must know," the old judge went on. "It wouldn't surprise me to see him in court again before long, on account of some brawl or other. He's possessed by a devil. The first time I cross-examined him he made a lunge at me, snatched away the book I was holding—a volume of the Code—and flung it into the wastepaper basket."

"Not a very polite gesture, I admit," said Andrea. "Still, as you say, it was aimed at the Code and not at you personally."

"So it was really an act of juridical criticism, you mean?" the old judge asked, laughing. "You're making fun of me, Signor Cipriani. Oh, well, that's hardly to be wondered at, seeing that I belong to the past and you to the present—or rather to the future, as you say. The fact remains that Sabatini continued to indulge in these violent outbreaks throughout his prison term, thereby earning the right to a couple of additional trials and extra stretches of solitary confinement. Did you know, by the way, that your friend's pardon was on the point of being refused because of his bad conduct record?"

"No, I didn't know that," Andrea confessed, "and frankly I'm amazed to hear it."

"Aha, you see? I told you you'd got Sabatini all wrong," the old judge declared with satisfaction. "That half-witted act of his gave me a lot of trouble at the trial, but, on my word, I've never felt any remorse about his conviction. It was never possible to clear up entirely the question of his probable accomplices or bosses, but that wasn't the court's fault—it was the stubbornness of your fellow villagers. I've devoted a whole page of my memoirs to this subject, and modesty apart I think I may claim . . ."

He paused and clasped his forehead in an effort to remember. Andrea tried in various ways to indicate that he was impatient to be alone with the documents, but the old judge, grappling with the mists of memory, paid no attention.

"Forgive me," he said at last, "it was all so long ago. . . . Yes, one day, in an attempt to break through the wall of silence that Sabatini had closed around him, I took the liberty of resorting to a somewhat unorthodox expedient, of which, consequently, you won't find any mention in the records. I pretended to allow Sabatini a private visit from his mother and the parish priest of Cisterna. I don't know if that reverend gentleman is still alive, by the way. . . ."

"Yes, he's still alive," said Andrea.

"A two-faced saint—that's what *he* is, let me tell you," said the old judge. "The three of them were left alone together in a little room, but I had instructed my clerk

74

and two policemen to eavesdrop outside the door. The first thing the prisoner did was to warn his visitors. 'Be on your guard,' he told them. 'The walls have ears.' Despite his warning, a few minutes later his mother asked him: 'If you agree, someone might testify on your behalf and say that he saw you that night.' 'No,' said the prisoner. The mother broke down and wept, but she didn't insist. What could her suggestion have meant? Was some accomplice willing to give false testimony? We never found out because the conversation became inaudible at that point, and we never succeeded in getting to the bottom of it."

"Are you sure that the parish priest of Cisterna was present?" Andrea asked.

"Positive," the old judge assured him. "In fact, I called him into my office. Without referring to the conversation we had just overheard, I suggested that he might preach a sermon on the Christian duty of testifying truthfully. He seemed greatly embarrassed and evasive. Actually, he said, the law had no jurisdiction over the pulpit. Actually, the only judgment of concern to a Christian was the judgment of God's Holy Tribunal. Well, that set off a full-scale row. After a while I lost my temper and accused him of withholding information. 'Do you realize,' I said to him, 'that suppressing the truth is the same as testifying falsely?' But of course the whole episode led to nothing. Certainly that priest knew a great deal, but I couldn't loosen his tongue. I heard afterward that the two Passionist Fathers who conducted the Lenten Mission in Cisterna that year had acted on my suggestion and exhorted 'whoever knew anything' to come forward and testify. But they were strangers, so nobody paid any attention to them. Believe me, Signor Cipriani, if that trial left certain questions unsolved, they concerned the situation and not the identity of the accused. What could I do? Arrest the whole village, beginning with the parish priest?"

"Why not?" said Andrea. "It's a pity you didn't."

"You'll find," the old judge rambled on, "that nearly every trial has some mysterious element. The fox is always careful to provide his lair with two entrances; but the skilled huntsman . . ."

Andrea was no longer listening. He glanced at his watch and murmured something about being late for an appointment. The old judge saw him out. As they parted, he said: "Do you want to give your—er—friend some useful advice, Signor Cipriani? Tell him to be content with his pardon; it's the most he can hope for, while I'm alive anyway."

CHAPTER EIGHT

THAT evening, Luca and Don Serafino set out from the village to meet Andrea, having had word that he was on his way back. He arrived on his motorcycle, as he had before, and they returned to the village together, Andrea walking beside his machine. Even after he had removed his dark goggles, he was almost unrecognizable under the thick layer of blackish dust that covered him. It had been a long ride.

"Let's go for a stroll," he suggested. "I feel like stretching my legs."

The inhabitants of Cisterna had not yet grown used to seeing them together. Every time it happened, people were surprised. Even the most charitable would gape as though they had landed from another planet. They had only to walk down the street for little groups of interested onlookers to form on every corner, while others, not quite so bold, peered out through the shutters, and mothers called their children to come indoors quickly. People referred to them, laconically, as "the friends." Don Serafino's shyness—which had to do only with his public

77

comportment—caused him acute embarrassment at such times, even though he tried to hide it.

"Shall we go round by the fields below the village, then?" he proposed. "Agreed? Let's not parade down the main street."

"You're ashamed to be seen with us," Andrea taunted him. "What's there to be ashamed about?"

"Don't start that again," the old priest remonstrated.

"Tell me if I'm right," Andrea insisted.

"Well, if you must know," Don Serafino retorted, "yes. And if you'd look in a mirror you'd see why."

Luca laughed. "*Pax vobiscum,*" he said.

Outwardly, if in no other way, Luca was the least eccentric of the company. Since his return, he had rested and cleaned up, and he now looked like a man who had retired from his job and was living, with gentle and serene good humor, on a pension—though a wretchedly small one. Not one of his contemporaries had spoken a word of welcome to this man released from life imprisonment for a crime of which he was innocent. Innocent? The word set the older villagers wrinkling skeptical noses. Innocent of what? The murder? Well, maybe, but as to the rest of it . . .

"Just here," said Luca to Andrea at a certain spot on the road, "there used to be an immensely tall poplar. You never saw it—I'm talking about fifty years ago. On a sunny day, we could tell the time by its shadow."

Luca's eyes moved slowly upward from the ground to the level of what once had been the treetop, reshaping the tree.

"Yes, indeed, it was our village clock," the priest agreed.

78

"Luca, do you remember the Showman? The one who got first prize for the best firework display in the diocese—what was his name?"

"Totonno," said Luca. "What a cheerful fellow he was."

"He was a friend of yours, wasn't he?" Don Serafino went on. "On feast days, after dark, he would light up that poplar like an altar."

"You see down there, where the pharmacy is?" said Luca to Andrea. "It used to be an empty field. Your father and I often played bowls there on a Sunday afternoon."

A group of young men, varying in age but all alike in their swarthy, sullen faces and their T-shirts, were lounging in front of a gasoline pump, arguing raucously about the Round-Italy bicycle race. Andrea asked one of them to keep an eye on his motorcycle.

Farther on there was the customary evening group of women with copper pitchers waiting to draw water from the fountain. As each one filled her pitcher, another would help her lift it and steady it on the round pad protecting her head. Under the weight of the brimming pitcher even the old women would tilt their chins and walk erect, so as not to spill the water. The approach of the three men surprised them. Their gabble subsided abruptly, but one voice rang out: "Ah, well, birds of a feather . . ." followed by a chorus of titters. Just then Andrea left his friends and strode toward the fountain. Afraid of being taken to task for their gibes, the women fled, squealing, their pitchers clanging. Andrea—who had merely wanted to wash his face and hands—had the fountain all to himself.

Don Serafino made another proposal.

"Let's go this way—it's a short cut," he said, determined that they should at least avoid the town hall.

"But that'll bring us round by the blind woman's balcony," Luca objected.

"What does that unhappy creature want of you?" Andrea asked. "Every time you go past her house, she makes a scene."

"She's a distant cousin of mine," Luca told him with some embarrassment.

Turning down a side street, the three friends found themselves at the back of the parish church just as the sacristy door opened to release the youngsters of the beginners' catechism class. Don Serafino was surrounded by a swarm of small figures eager to kiss his hand. Luca's eyes, as he watched them, were filled with tenderness.

"But where are our children?" he murmured to Andrea.

Andrea was more touched by this than Luca could have imagined, but all he said was: "Haven't we got Toni?"

Luca's face lit up as he answered:

"I'll tell him that—it'll make him happy."

Suddenly, unexpectedly, someone called Luca by name. He saw an old cripple huddled against the sacristy wall. The man was ragged and filthy, like a beggar, and the look on his face was at once humble and depraved.

"Don't you recognize me?" he croaked.

Luca looked at him intently.

"No," he said. "I'm sorry, but I don't remember you."

"Ah, well, a lot of time has gone by since we were in the army together at Ancona. You don't remember?"

"The corporal! I'll be damned!" exclaimed Luca. "You don't seem to be in too good shape."

"Could I have a word with you?" the corporal asked him.

"Go on ahead," Luca told his friends. "I'll join you in a moment."

The two walked on slowly as far as the little square in front of the school.

"Let's sit down here, otherwise Luca won't find us," said Don Serafino. "I'm glad that people are finally beginning to speak to him."

In the middle of the square there was a miserable, dusty little garden, with a few stunted trees, a rotting wooden bench, and an enormous, ancient urinal scribbled over with obscene drawings.

"Is this where you want to wait?" Andrea asked with a grimace of disgust. "No, I've a better idea, since we've got the chance. Come."

Without waiting for a reply, he strode forward down a steep lane that led out of the village, and the priest had no choice but to follow him. The lane was flanked by stables, pigsties and wooden hovels roofed with sheets of tin. The wretched occupants sat in the doorways eating their evening soup, or simply getting a breath of cool air.

"Where the devil are you taking me?" the priest panted as Andrea, ahead of him, quickened his pace.

But Andrea said nothing. As soon as they left the village, the lane dwindled to a narrow path between high, thorny hedgerows.

81

"How's Luca going to find us here?" Don Serafino protested.

"He won't," said Andrea. "For once I want him to lose track of us."

The priest frowned and refused to go any farther.

"Come on," Andrea ordered. "I've got to talk to you about him. Seriously, I mean, this time."

More than the words themselves, the tone in which they were spoken put Don Serafino on his guard.

"My poor friend," he said, "this is really becoming an obsession with you."

"You're perfectly right," Andrea agreed. "It's an obsession. Try as I may, I can think of nothing else. Well, I'm sorry, but I've got a few embarrassing questions to ask you."

"Take my advice, Andrea—forget about it," the priest entreated him. "Believe me, it would be better."

"Better for whom? For your own peace of mind?"

"Andrea, my heart still bleeds at certain desolate memories. Surely they should be treated with some respect?"

"If these memories are still bleeding," said Andrea, "it's unhygienic to cover them up with dirty bandages."

The old priest stiffened, as though struck across the face.

"What makes you say 'dirty'?" he demanded. "Are you speaking of me?"

Andrea evaded a direct reply.

"Christ," he exclaimed, "can't I know why so many people in Cisterna are afraid of Luca? Why no one dares talk about his trial?"

"Don't change the subject," Don Serafino enjoined him sharply. "Answer me: do you believe I could ever have had any reason for wanting Luca to be convicted?"

"Well, to be frank, I don't feel too happy about you," Andrea admitted. "We might as well talk about it openly. Come on, let's walk a little farther."

The path emerged into open country, with fields and orchards on either side, and suddenly the air was filled with a pungent fragrance of peppers and new-mown hay. The two men sat down on the grassy verge of the path.

"A few days ago," Andrea began, "I had occasion to go to Aquila. It's not a very big place, as I hardly need remind you. The whole life of the town centers round one arcade fifty yards long. There I ran into the crown prosecutor. We started talking, one thing led to another, to Cisterna and then to Luca Sabatini. He saw my interest in Luca's case, and gave me an introduction to an older colleague, now retired, who'd been prosecutor during that iniquitous trial at the Assizes where Luca was convicted."

"That odious bloodhound!" the priest commented. "Is he still alive?"

"He hasn't forgotten you either," said Andrea. "He mentioned the behavior of the Cisterna people, parish priest included, in connection with that trial. He told me certain very disturbing details, if they're true."

"What could he have told you?" Don Serafino protested. "The idiot couldn't make head or tail of that trial, let me tell you. All he could do was scrabble at it, like a chicken in the straw. As if reeling off page after page of laws, statutes and by-laws could have got him anywhere

83

with a man like Luca. The whole performance was absurd
—grotesque."

"I can well believe it," said Andrea, "but just now I'm
interested in something else. It appears—if the old judge
didn't misinform me—that you visited Luca in prison while
he was awaiting trial."

"Yes, I went with his mother," said Don Serafino. "Poor
Teresa wasn't in a fit state to make the journey alone. She
was like Mary on Calvary."

"That meeting was a rather important one, wasn't it?
Decisive, even, in a sense?"

"In what sense?"

"You don't remember what you talked about with Luca?
I mean, in connection with the trial?"

"No. How could I, after all these years?"

"I don't believe you," said Andrea curtly.

Pale with indignation, Don Serafino turned on him.

"How dare you?" he exclaimed. "You're cross-examin-
ing me now just like that fool of a prosecutor."

"There's a difference," said Andrea with an ironical
smile. "He wanted to convict a living man by means of a
printed book. I don't want to convict anyone—neither you
nor anyone else. I only want to understand."

Don Serafino stood up and glanced around, as though
to see whether anyone was coming. He was bathed in
sweat and gasping for breath. He took off his hat and
mopped his forehead with a large handkerchief.

"Shout if you like," Andrea told him. "No one will hear
you."

"Andrea, is this supposed to be a joke? What are you
trying to get out of me?"

"The truth—that's all. Now answer me. Why did you refuse when the prosecutor asked you to warn your congregation from the pulpit that anyone who knew anything about Luca's case was in duty bound to come forward?"

Don Serafino, livid and trembling, stammered: "Andrea, don't be absurd. You're not my bishop."

With this, he turned and began to walk back in the direction of the village. But Andrea at one bound seized him by the shoulder.

"You won't escape," he said. "I'm stronger than you, and I can run faster. It's true I'm not your bishop, but I'm a friend of Luca's, and I insist on knowing to what extent you were implicated in the great misfortune of his life."

"Have you lost your mind?" cried Don Serafino in a voice that betrayed his panic. "Ask Luca himself and you'll hear what he has to say to such bullying."

"Luca is too good," said Andrea. "But even if he has forgiven and forgotten, I, as his friend, can never forgive the person who did him such irreparable harm. So listen to what I'm going to say, and answer me honestly. While you were in that room, talking to Luca, an employee of the court was listening at the door. He reported that there was someone, here in Cisterna, whose testimony would have been enough to acquit Luca. This potential witness was apparently quite willing to come forward. He may even have been waiting in the building at that very moment."

"Very well," said the priest, "if you know that much, you might as well know the rest. You might as well know it was Luca himself who forbade it."

"Aha, I'm glad to see your memory is returning,"

Andrea remarked caustically. "But why did you need his permission? Wasn't it your duty to protect him, to rescue him, even against his will? If you saw a man trying to commit suicide, would you rush to save him, or would you wait to consult him first?"

"Can't you see"—Don Serafino's breathing had become so difficult that he could speak only with an effort—"can't you see that according to your argument the first person to blame would be his mother? If poor Teresa respected her son's wish, don't you think she may have known the reason for it and felt, in her heart of hearts, that he was right?"

"His mother was a good Christian woman," said Andrea. "She was a faithful churchgoer. If she resigned herself to such an inhuman situation, it must have been out of obedience to you. At the very least you must know something about it."

Frightened, haggard, Don Serafino again tried to escape, but Andrea gripped his arm.

"For Christ's sake," Andrea exclaimed, shaking him roughly, "don't force me to strike you. I assure you I'm capable of it. Your cassock wouldn't stop me. I'd have done it already, if it weren't for your age. But don't think you can trade on that indefinitely. My patience has a limit."

"You're mad, you're mad," the old priest repeated with tears in his eyes. "In all my life I've never been treated like this."

Andrea was unmoved. There was a ruthless ferocity in his face.

"The person willing to testify in Luca's favor," he demanded. "Who was he? And what was the evidence that would have proved his innocence?"

"Be quiet," the priest said. "Here he comes."

"I'll ask him to go away and leave us alone," Andrea declared firmly. "I'm not letting you off this time."

Luca was striding rapidly toward them, followed by an enormous sheepdog that kept barking and jumping at his heels.

"Listen," Don Serafino murmured to Andrea, his chin quivering, "I'll come and talk with you this evening, after dinner—I promise."

"You both look ghastly," Luca exclaimed as he caught up with them. "What's happened?"

"What did that corporal want?" Andrea asked.

"A small loan," Luca told him with a smile.

CHAPTER NINE

SOME peasants were breaking up the stony ground on the slope of the hill. The topsoil was dried out and barren, and they had to dig deep to find the loam. Nothing grew on the hill except a few scrawny fruit trees. Catching sight of Andrea, one of the peasants—a young man, naked to the waist, his face flushed crimson beneath unruly black hair—planted his pickaxe in the ground and ran smiling to meet him.

"Are you coming to our meeting tonight?" he asked Andrea eagerly.

"Yes, of course. I promised you I would," Andrea told him.

"We hardly ever see you. . . ."

"You must forgive me, I'm still busy on something. . . . It's rather difficult to explain."

"We'd like to hear you explain about the problems," the young man went on, overcoming his shyness.

"Which problems?"

"Well—the problems of freedom. We'd like a chance to ask you questions."

"I promise you I'll be there, as early as I can manage," said Andrea, clasping his hand.

The young peasant went back to his digging.

"He's a queer bird all right," remarked one of the others, following Andrea with his eyes.

"He had the whole countryside in the palm of his hand," said the third, "but he's been acting so strangely that it's slipping through his fingers."

"If he won't get jobs for people, he won't get any votes at the next election," added the first.

"He's not going to run for office," said the young one. "He's not looking for votes."

"Then what is he looking for?"

"Freedom. He wants the workers to be free."

"What does that mean? That they'll put through the railroad? Every now and then they talk about it. On the eve of every election they talk about it."

"The railroad has nothing to do with it," the young man retorted. "He'll tell you what it means."

Andrea crossed the patch of grass outside the little rustic chapel of San Silvestro, goal of the yearly springtime Rogation pilgrimage. He paused for a moment on the wooden footbridge that spanned a narrow trickle of water —the Hare's Bridge, people called it. He recalled the memorable occasion when, as a small boy, he had taken part in the Rogation rites, and suddenly, before the eyes of the assembled worshipers, a hare appeared, right on the bridge. The worshipers, in less time than it takes to tell, set candles and crucifix on the ground and were off in full cry after the luckless animal. They surrounded it, they closed in on it from all sides; but the hare eluded them; it disappeared into thin air. Don Serafino maintained it had surely been an apparition of the Devil. His pronouncement caused a sensation. Why did the Devil show such an interest in this particular spot? It was here, a few years earlier, that Luca's troubles had begun. It was here that they had arrested him at dawn. The night before a merchant had been killed in his carriage, a mile or so down the main road.

Beside the bridge there was a dam which, when the mill was working, had diverted the stream. Andrea followed the path along the bank of the old millrace, now overgrown with weeds, until he reached the mill. It was a low, wide building, two stories high, with a front yard where carts and animals had once gathered, bringing grain to the mill or loading flour. The yard was girdled with tall poplars; beyond them ran the stream. A donkey stood tethered to one of the poplars; close by a goat browsed.

Old Ludovico sat leaning against the doorpost, dazed and motionless. Agnese, his wife, darted back and forth near the doorway in a fury mixed with panic.

"What do you want here?" she stormed at the visitor before he could open his mouth.

"Didn't Don Serafino tell you?" Andrea asked. "He must have told you why I was coming."

"When we need the priest we go to church," the old woman retorted, going back into the house. "We're under our own roof here," she screamed from inside.

"I've come to have a talk with you," said Andrea to Ludovico. "Yes, I mean you."

The old man looked at him in terror, as if Andrea had uttered some dreadful threat.

"I've got nothing to say to you," he stammered. "I know nothing. Go away."

"If your memory needs jogging, I can jog it," Andrea informed him in a tone that was far from reassuring. "You know perfectly well what I've come to talk to you about, and I'm not leaving until you've told me everything."

"I know nothing," the old man repeated in a quavering voice. "Nothing."

Andrea moved closer to him and tried peaceful persuasion.

"Listen," he said. "Our families have always been neighborly. Why should we quarrel?"

It was like talking to a stone. Ludovico paid no attention.

"Do you hear me?" Andrea demanded, raising his voice. "Do you hear me?"

Old Agnese reappeared in the doorway.

"Are you still here?" she screeched, baring her teeth in rage. "What do you want? Are we no longer masters in our own home?"

"Be quiet, you old witch," Andrea snapped. "So you won't talk? Idiots—that's what you are. If you don't quit, I may have to change my plans, and ask you for an accounting in certain matters. That would be far worse for both of you."

These words—either because they were unexpected or because they were dreaded—produced a certain effect. Ludovico slowly raised his great head and peered at Andrea through half-closed eyes, like an owl flinching from the light.

"I don't understand," he said.

"What impudence," Andrea answered. "By this time your donkey would know what I'm talking about."

"People don't like to be disturbed in their own home," Agnese put in whiningly.

"Their own home?" Andrea repeated with a mocking smile. "So you think the papers of a certain mortgage don't exist any more? You think they got lost or burned just because, in all the years I've been away, I never asked you for any payments? But never mind that. That's not what I've come for."

Perhaps to give them time to think, he moved off and began to stroll around the mill, but he must also have looked to them like a creditor legitimately entitled to inspect his property. He could hear them conferring—bickering—in an undertone.

A majestic walnut tree, recently felled, sprawled in its death agony on the slope of the waterfall behind the mill, the trunk intact, but the great branches shattered, the torn roots seeming to bleed in the deep hollow hacked out by the blows of the axe. At Andrea's approach, a flock of sparrows rose from the tangled mass of branches. The sky was pale, monotonous, indifferent.

Slowly Andrea walked back to the yard, where he found the old couple even more crestfallen than before.

"I didn't mean to frighten you," he said in an attempt to soothe them. "That's why I asked Don Serafino to let you know I was coming. For Christ's sake, I'm not trying to harm you!"

"Our two families have always lived in peace," sighed the old man. "For my part . . ."

"But when you're poor, everything frightens you," wailed the old woman. "A dog that's been beaten is afraid of the baker's shovel or the priest's holy water."

Agnese whimpered tearfully for a while; entreating the Madonna: "Our Lady of Loreto, help me," she repeated. "Our Lady of Pratola, help me." Then she dried her eyes on her apron. All of a sudden, as though remembering a matter of the utmost urgency, she dashed into the house to fetch a chair for Andrea.

"I'm sorry," she said. "Would you like a glass of wine? You know, I never forget your father and mother when I pray for the souls of the dead."

Like some harried animal, eyes bloodshot beneath reddened lids, Ludovico kept glancing right and left along the ground.

"You see what we're reduced to?" he said. "I've worked all my life, night and day, since I was twelve years old. You see what we're reduced to?"

Andrea sat down beside him.

"I had the mill and they forced me to close it," Ludovico went on lamenting. "I owned a fifth of the forest; it was burned to ashes. I had . . ."

"I hope you're not trying to blame Luca for all this," Andrea broke in.

"And what if I am?"

"Oh, come, don't be absurd. You know very well that he was in prison."

"Yes, but his sin was here."

"What sin?"

"It was here, I tell you, like the plague, like a cancer—in the air, in the ground.

"Listen," said Andrea, "I don't want to waste your time. Now tell me what you know about Luca's trial."

"Again?" cried Agnese. "That trial? Are they going to dig it up again? Will it never end?"

"Now that this cursed business has cropped up again, people have been looking at me queerly," muttered Ludovico. "Are we back at the beginning?"

"No one's going to reopen the case," Andrea assured them. "Luca has been pardoned, and that's enough for him. He doesn't care about being vindicated. You know what he's like—or at least you ought to. But I'm a very different sort of person, even though I happen to be his friend. I need to understand what happened. And where Luca is concerned, I still don't understand."

Agnese stared at her husband, and her whole body trembled in her anxiety for him. Ludovico said nothing, but stared at the ground in a state of imbecile abstraction.

"Did you hear me?" Andrea demanded.

Finally the old man looked up.

"What do you want to understand?" he asked. "That accursed trial? No one has ever been able to understand it."

"Did you know that Luca was innocent?" Andrea asked.

"Only Jesus Christ is innocent," Ludovico answered piously.

"Stop quibbling. You know very well what I mean. Were you or weren't you aware that Luca was innocent of the murder for which he was convicted?"

"Everyone knew he was innocent of the murder," said Ludovico. "More or less."

94

"What do you mean, everyone?" Andrea exclaimed. "Even the jury?"

"I think so."

"And the judges?"

"Of course. Judges aren't all that stupid."

"Then how do you explain their convicting him?"

"They had to convict someone. A man had been murdered. Luca was the accused."

"Why did they pick Luca instead of someone else— you, for instance, or my father?"

"Why should they accuse us? We were at home, minding our own business."

"And Luca wasn't?"

"Apparently not. If he'd been home, they wouldn't have accused him."

"What was he doing if he wasn't minding his own business?"

"He certainly knows the answer better than I do. Why don't you ask him? He's your friend, isn't he. You're always together."

"Well, at least tell me how you explain his getting life imprisonment when everyone knew he was innocent."

"He lost the case. That always happens when the defendant loses the case. You're a schoolmaster, you ought to know these things better than I do."

"Ludovico, don't keep trying to wriggle out of it."

The old man sweated and groaned. His words came convulsively, in an almost incomprehensible dialect. Agnese watched him with compassion, and suffered for them both.

"Ludovico, try to answer straight," Andrea persisted, looming over him. "Isn't it possible that Luca lost the case because someone who could have given evidence in his favor held back from doing it?"

Ludovico closed his eyes and said nothing.

"Are you feeling sick?" Agnese asked him.

"He's feeling perfectly all right," Andrea assured her. Then he turned again to Ludovico. "Did you understand my question?"

"I understood it, all right," Ludovico answered, looking up at him with the eyes of a beaten dog. "I understood it. But what in the name of God is the use of asking it? Why do you want to rip open old wounds?"

"Never mind about that," Andrea told him. "So it's true, is it, that you were one of the people who had proof of Luca's innocence?"

"Only Jesus Christ is innocent," Ludovico repeated.

"I'm not talking about Original Sin," said Andrea, at the end of his patience. "I'm talking about the murder for which Luca was wrongly convicted. You knew he was innocent."

Ludovico responded with an almost imperceptible nod.

"You knew that Luca was somewhere else that night at the time of the murder?"

Again the old man nodded slowly.

"That was the Devil's night," he murmured.

"Tell him everything you know," his wife implored him. "If you don't, they may think we were guilty, poor innocents that we are."

"I saw Luca that night," said Ludovico in a faint voice. "But that's all. I know nothing about anything else, so help me God."

96

"Go on," his wife urged. "Tell him how it happened that you saw him. Maybe they'll suspect us if you keep silent now."

"All right, you start," Ludovico told her angrily. "Wasn't it you that woke me?"

Andrea turned to Agnese.

"Don't be afraid," he said.

The old woman made the sign of the cross.

"Yes, it was my fault," she began. "Even now I don't know which was at my elbow—the Blessed Virgin or Satan himself. It's hard to understand anything about that terrible night. It was a Friday eve."

"That's not important. Go on."

"Thursday evening Ludovico and I went to bed later than usual. We had killed the pig and we'd stayed up working on it, salting the lard and the hams. I was very tired, so I fell asleep right away. I'm such a sound sleeper that, even without being tired, I'd have slept through cannon fire. Millers don't notice noise—it's a well-known fact. But that night I woke with a start, somewhere in the small hours, and I woke my husband. I'd had a terrible dream—indeed, it wasn't like a dream at all, it was more like a vision. I'd seen Luca throwing himself into the canal. I'd seen him struggle desperately in the depths of the water. I'd heard him shout and cry out to me for help. The same thing had already happened several times before, with other people. . . ."

"Only once," Ludovico amended.

"You're forgetting the Showman," Agnese reminded him. "The year before, the Showman threw himself in."

"Only once," Ludovico insisted.

"You're forgetting the shepherd's wife," said Agnese. "That was about ten years earlier, the year we got married."

"It doesn't matter," Andrea interrupted. "Carry on. I don't want to hear about the others."

"I woke my husband and I told him my dream," Agnese continued. "I was nearly out of my wits with terror. Nobody ever gets that frightened by an ordinary dream. But that's just it—it was no dream. 'Mother of God, have mercy on us,' I prayed at the top of my voice. 'Holy Virgin, have mercy on us.' "

"She was nearly out of her wits, all right," Ludovico agreed. "Many's the time I've seen her in a state about something, but never the way she was that night. You'd think she was having convulsions. It was plain there was only one way to calm her down—I'd have to get up and go and take a look. A fine prospect. It was the middle of winter, and a north wind was blowing that made the entire mill hiss like a nest of serpents. I took my greatcoat, and a stick with an iron tip, and I lit a lantern."

"It wasn't till I saw him going out that the fear began to let go of me," Agnese resumed. "I got up and wrapped myself in the eiderdown and stood at the window, watching him. The sky was black as pitch, but there was some snow on the ground, so you could see a little."

"Understand, indeed!" Ludovico broke in, turning to Andrea. "You talk about wanting to understand, but I tell you, no one ever understood what really happened on that infernal night."

98

"Go ahead, please," Andrea told him. "What did you see?"

"Wait a minute," said the old man. "Where was I? Oh, yes, as I was saying, I took my stick and the lantern and I went downstairs. The moment I put my nose outside the door, with the cold nearly taking my breath away, the chimes of the belfry clock came to me on the wind. It was three in the morning, an hour only fit for wolves. I started out from the waterfall, here behind the house, and began walking slowly along the path by the canal, toward the dam. There was a thin sheet of ice on the water; anyone throwing himself in would have left a hole. I held my lantern up, trying to search the canal, and I kept my ears pricked for the slightest sound. Even the sleet was frozen underfoot, and I had to take care not to slip and fall into the water myself. I'd walked some distance and was just beginning to wonder if there was any use in going on, when I noticed a shadow leaning against a poplar tree. What could any man be doing at such an hour, in such a place? I looked back at the house and saw a light at the upstairs window and my wife's form behind the pane. That made me feel better, bold enough to face the shadow. I could see it was a man of medium height, muffled up in a greatcoat like my own. He was leaning with his back against the poplar and staring into the canal. 'Hey, who are you?' I shouted at him. 'What are you doing here at this hour?' He turned his head slowly toward me, but he didn't answer. Then I went closer, and saw that it was Luca. He looked ready to collapse; I think that if it hadn't been for the tree, he'd have fallen flat on the ground.

99

"To tell you the truth," the old man went on, "there had never been much love lost between us. Of late, we'd hardly spoken. But I couldn't help feeling worried when I saw him there at that hour of night, especially after Agnese's dream. 'Luca,' I said, 'what are you doing here? Are you sick? Don't you want to go home? Will you come back to the mill with me for a hot drink?' He didn't answer. He didn't say anything for a little while. Then he asked: 'What time is it?' 'It's just struck three,' I told him. 'Luca, do you realize that it's three o'clock and you ought to be asleep?' 'Forgive me,' he said, 'do you mean three in the afternoon or three in the morning?' That shows you how clouded his brain was. His voice was very faint, but otherwise it hadn't changed—I mean he hadn't been drinking or anything like that. I did my best to make him come away, I tried to insist, but it was no good. 'Leave me alone,' he said, and that was all. It seemed plain to me that, if he'd really intended to jump into the canal, he'd have done it by that time, and if for some reason he just wanted to go on standing there, well, at the very worst, I thought, he'd catch pneumonia. So I stopped worrying and went home."

"Of course, it would have been better if he had forced Luca to come back to the mill," said Agnese. "But how were we to know? I'd been able to keep track of my husband's course from the little window of our bedroom, thanks to his lantern. The window faced north, and blasts of air as sharp as knives came through the shutters. I've never been able to get rid of the rheumatism I caught that night. I kept my eyes fixed on the lantern, and at a certain point I too noticed the black shadow leaning against the

100

poplar. When Ludovico got back, the first thing I did was to ask him: 'Who is it?' 'It's Luca,' he told me. So it was the man who'd begged me for help in my dream. 'Why did you leave him standing there?' I said to my husband. 'What was I supposed to do?' said he. 'Take him on my back and carry him?'"

"Well," Ludovico put in sulkily, "how was anyone to guess that a murder was being committed at that very moment, practically under our noses?"

"My husband went back to bed," Agnese continued, "but I couldn't tear myself away from the window; I couldn't take my eyes off that shadow by the poplar. Somehow I just couldn't feel easy about him. I began to say the rosary. The way my heart was pounding, it really hurt. And all the time there was a fear growing inside me—I don't know the words to describe it. I felt that something terrible was happening, something I couldn't understand. I kept saying over and over to myself: 'Holy Mary, Mother of God.' I've no idea how long I stood there."

"It was a cursedly long night," said Ludovico. "I woke up suddenly I don't know how many times, and every time it was still night."

"There was never a night as long as that one," Agnese went on. "The day just wouldn't come. But finally, after a long time, I saw the shadow move away from the tree. I woke my husband at once. The sky had paled a little; it must have been nearly dawn. We stood together and watched Luca walking toward the dam, on his way back to the village. 'Thank God,' I said to my husband. 'He's

101

not going to kill himself after all. The Blessed Virgin was protecting him.'"

"What time would that have been?" Andrea asked.

"A little before five," said Ludovico.

"It wasn't light enough to be five," Agnese contradicted him.

"It was winter," Ludovico retorted crossly. "That's why the dawn was late. No sooner were we back in bed than the north wind brought us the belfry chimes. There were five strokes. I can hear them still. The sun never rose again for Luca, but it began to set for others too. You can see for yourself how we've been ruined—ruined by the curse."

"Was Luca arrested right away?" Andrea asked.

"Right away," said Ludovico. "At the Hare's Bridge."

"Someone brought word to the police," said Agnese, "that a man had been robbed and killed in his carriage on the Avezzano road, an hour or two earlier. A search party started out, and the first person they met was Luca's mother, Teresa. 'My son didn't come home last night,' she told the sergeant. 'I was wondering if you might have arrested him for drunkenness.' Presently they saw Luca returning to the village. He was dirty, and he was numb with cold, and a bit dazed, too—the way anyone would be after spending a night in the open, in mid-winter. Right there in front of his mother, they asked him where he'd been. 'That's no concern of yours,' he answered, and he kept on saying it till the day he was convicted."

"But why couldn't he tell them where he'd spent the night?" said Andrea in amazement. "It might have

102

sounded strange, but there was nothing to be ashamed of. Why didn't he name you as a witness?"

"Ask him that yourself," said Ludovico peevishly. "You're always together."

"But you—you?" Andrea insisted. "Why didn't you come forward at once and tell what you knew? Your testimony alone would have been enough to save him."

"Luca wouldn't have it," Agnese burst out. "That's the truth."

"But why?" Andrea repeated.

"I don't know," said Ludovico.

"Do you think he's a madman?"

"No."

"Then there must be some reason. How do you explain it?"

"I've told you my side of it," the old man answered. "The rest doesn't concern me. You can't ask a donkey to do the work of an ox."

"Do you really want to know all of it?" Agnese put in abruptly. "Do you want me to tell you everything there is to tell? At a certain point in this affair, it became crystal clear that everyone—everyone, mind you—might as well give up trying to understand it. It had become a private question between God and the Devil."

"And as usual," Ludovico murmured, "the Devil won."

"Never mind that now," said Andrea irritably. "I'm not asking you to go into it that deeply. All I want you to do is answer a few simple questions."

"More questions?" groaned Ludovico in desperation.

"Why didn't you come forward at the trial?"

"Answer him," Agnese urged. "If you don't answer, he may think it was your fault."

"When the prosecutor sent for Luca's mother, Teresa, to come to Aquila with Don Serafino, who was still the parish priest," said Ludovico, "I went along, too. As soon as we arrived, they brought me to a tavern and left me there. 'Don't move,' the priest told me. 'Don't speak to anyone. If they ask what you're doing here, tell them some lie or other.' I ate and slept in that tavern and never once set foot outside it, not even for fresh air. They didn't return till the following day. The mother, poor woman, was in such a state I thought her last hour had come. 'There's nothing to do,' she said. 'You may go now,' the priest told me. 'You may go home. Don't breathe a word to anyone about your coming here.' So all that happened was that I was stuck for my traveling expenses."

"The whole affair had passed beyond human control," Agnese said. "Do you see what I mean? It no longer had anything to do with judges or witnesses or relatives."

"Might I take a look out of that upstairs window?" Andrea asked. "Just to get an idea."

Agnese rose and led the way into the house. They climbed the steep, narrow stairway to the upper floor.

"This is the window," the old woman told him. "You see that willow tree over there? That's just about the spot where the poplar used to be—the one he leaned against."

CHAPTER TEN

CISTERNA and Perticara are two big villages,
lying on either slope of the same mountain, completely
hidden from each other; but the distance between them can
be covered, at a leisurely walk, in less than an hour. On
the evening before his arrest, Luca had attended a family
reunion at the home of his betrothed in Perticara. Page
after page of the court record was devoted to this gathering. Everyone who had been there had been cross-examined
several times, and the prosecutor had leaned heavily on
their statements in preparing his summing-up. And most
of the notes Andrea made while going through the documents concerned that evening.

Luca had been engaged to the Perticara girl for almost
two years, and this family party ought to have proved a
happy occasion for him, too. Instead, things had taken a
very different turn. After some confused explanations
which made everyone think he was leading up to yet another plea for postponing the wedding, and which later,
in the police reports, assumed an ominous significance,
Luca had ended by imploring the girl to break off their
engagement.

105

"Today I'm going to Perticara," Andrea told Don Serafino. "I've already sent word to a friend of mine there."

"Waste of time," the priest commented.

"You felt the same way about my visit to Ludovico; nevertheless, I got him to talk."

"That was a miracle if ever there was one. Miracles don't happen every day, though. . . . Tell me, are you being looked after properly at your cousin's place?"

"Don't change the subject. You'll see. I'll get everything out of you, too."

"You flatter yourself."

"I'll get the very stones to talk."

Andrea was standing by the window in Don Serafino's study, his hands in his pockets, his face pale, brooding.

"Frankly, Andrea, I'm disappointed in you," the priest said. "I thought you were a socialist. I thought you were tackling all sorts of present-day problems. Instead you seem to have developed a mania for archaeology."

"So you consider yourself a museum piece?"

"Luca's getting suspicious, you know. These trips you keep taking, all on your own, without saying a word to him . . ."

"I hope that doesn't mean you've been talking too much. You might at least play fair in that respect."

"But can't you be satisfied with what you've already found out from Ludovico? Isn't it enough to know for certain that Luca is innocent?"

"I've been convinced of Luca's innocence from the time I was eight years old. The thing that baffles me is this village."

"It's your own village. You were born and bred here."

106

"I just can't make it out. You unravel one secret, and there's another secret behind it. You pull aside one veil and find a thicker one. Believe me, I'll never have any peace until I understand it."

"There's nothing to understand. You're wasting your time."

Andrea stopped his motorcycle outside the town hall in the little market square of Perticara. He was instantly surrounded by an eager crowd, which grew bigger as people poured out of the little shops of every kind surrounding the square and even out of the town hall itself, its ancient façade plastered with campaign posters. Among them one poster stood out, the size of a sheet, with the slogan in red: UNCLE JOE IS COMING.

A tall young man in blue overalls elbowed his way forward through the crowd. Andrea hailed him.

"I've told Gelsomina," the young man said, laughing. "She's expecting you."

"Who's Gelsomina?"

"She's poor Lauretta's sister—the only one of the family left. Come on, I'll take you to her."

"Does she know why I'm here? You must have had a hard time persuading her to see me."

"Gelsomina? Heavens, no. She's a comrade. She runs our co-operative store. It'll be an honor for her. In any case, she probably knows you already."

They turned down a narrow, stony lane between blackened, ancient houses, dwellings and stables intermingled. A pungent smell of sheep came from the houses, of cheese

107

laid out to dry in wicker baskets, and of curds simmering in vats. The co-operative store was at the other end of the lane, where the houses clung to the craggy slope of the mountain. The front of the store had been newly white-washed. In the doorway stood an elderly woman, vigorous-looking, wearing a grease-spattered white apron over her black dress.

"This is Gelsomina," Andrea's guide told him. "I'm leaving you in good hands—I must be off; I've got a truck to repair. See you later."

"Comrade Cipriani," said Gelsomina, holding out her hand, "we've met before."

"Yes, so we have," Andrea answered with a smile. "I remember perfectly. Weren't you standing next to me at the party reception in the town hall?"

"You've a good memory. . . . How nice to have a chance of talking to you at last."

"I must say, though, that I'd never have thought that Sunday that the comrade standing beside me . . ."

". . . would turn out to be Lauretta's sister? Well, no more would I have guessed that you might be a friend of Luca's. Upon my word, the more I think about that, the less I understand it. I think about it quite a lot, you know. Comrade Cipriani, do you want me to tell you the truth? I'm ashamed to confess it—I know it's against all party principles—but the fact is, I can think of nothing else."

"Well, now we can talk about it in peace and quiet. That's precisely why I'm here."

"Is Luca in the party too? He isn't? Thank goodness for that. But I mustn't keep you standing at the door.

108

Please come in. Business is slack at this time of day, and I've got a little room of my own behind the shop. I'll make some coffee, or would you rather have a glass of wine?"

"What wine have you got?"

"Apulian—black."

"Coffee, then."

The shop was a poor, rustic little place, with a floor of beaten earth, unplastered walls made of stones and rocks and a bare framework of cane instead of a roof. The range of merchandise was limited: macaroni, olive oil, dried codfish, rope, sulfur and soap. There was a chest of glass-fronted drawers for the different kinds of macaroni, and above it hung two colored chromos: one of Karl Marx, great head and tawny lion's mane; the other of our Saviour, red-robed, preaching the Sermon on the Mount. "Blessed are they that thirst for justice" was the caption underneath.

Gelsomina's room was a dank cave hollowed out of the living rock. It smelled abominably of dried codfish, but the cool dusk was pleasant. The scant daylight of the lane was filtered by a close-meshed curtain hanging in the entrance to keep out the flies. But one soon grew accustomed to the darkness. A spirit lamp standing in a niche hewn in the rock gave the cave the look of a kitchen. While Gelsomina was making the coffee, Andrea's eyes strayed to a portrait on the wall. It was the photograph of a young girl dressed in the fashion of a bygone day. Beneath a heavy mass of hair coiled on top of her head, two great frightened eyes stared out of a pale, thin little face. There was something hallucinatory and phantomlike about the portrait, but this might simply have been due to the inexpertness of the photographer. A knot of black crape on one corner of the frame left Andrea in no doubt.

"Lauretta?" he asked.

Gelsomina nodded, and her eyes filled instantly with tears.

"She was a lily," she said. "How can I describe her to you? She never journeyed beyond this mountain where she was born. Trains, ships, seaports, railway stations, theaters were all sinful words to her."

"How did she die?"

"Of a sickness you can't find in the medical books." Then Gelsomina added: "Three months after the trial."

A saucerful of cheese rinds stood on the floor in a corner of the cave.

"There's a mouse that I have to bribe every day," the woman explained. "His part of the bargain is to keep away from the food in the shop."

"You talk as though you knew him personally."

"Well, I do. But he never comes out when I have visitors."

"That's a pity," Andrea said. "I'd have liked to ask his opinion."

"About what? About me?"

"No, about the people hereabouts."

"He doesn't know anyone but me," Gelsomina declared complacently.

She served the coffee in two tiny cups, the size of thimbles, and sat down opposite her guest. Her face contrasted curiously with her opulent bosom and masses of shining, carefully-oiled gray hair. It was a small face, as wizened as an old potato, its features sharpened by a lifetime of solitary hardship, yet deep in her eyes one could see a sheeplike melancholy and mildness.

"You have the same way of doing your hair," observed Andrea, with a glance in the direction of her sister's photograph.

"Maybe it doesn't suit me," she conceded, "but I do it that way in memory of her."

"It suits you perfectly," Andrea assured her. Then, abruptly changing his tone, he went on: "Tell me, how would you feel about seeing Luca again? Don't think the suggestion comes from him. He doesn't even know I'm here today, and if he did know he certainly wouldn't like it."

Gelsomina's body stiffened in a spasm.

"As for seeing him again," she said, when she had regained her composure, "I've already seen him. Wasn't it Luca you were with, last Sunday morning, near Don Serafino's house?"

"Why didn't you come up and speak to him? I don't know what wrongs he may have done your family, but you must admit he has paid dearly for them."

"I don't know if it's of any interest to you, Comrade Cipriani, but the fact is I'd gone to Cisterna simply and solely to have a word with you. Then I saw you with him, and it gave me such a fright I couldn't stop trembling. So I came straight home without once turning round."

"I'm sorry. What did you want to speak to me about?"

"I just wanted to talk to you. I wanted your advice and help."

"Thank you. You can't imagine how flattered that makes me feel."

"For forty years, Comrade Cipriani, I've lived with this sword piercing my heart. As time went by, I got used to it; I thought it was my fate. But now that he's been set free, some people think he's innocent, and to crown everything, he's a friend of yours. Does that mean we're back at the beginning. I can feel the rusty old sword twisting around in my heart again, tearing it to shreds, the old scar beginning to bleed again—a hemorrhage that will not stop. I can't describe the torment."

"Luca is a good man, Gelsomina. He really is. He doesn't deserve to be hated or feared."

"Comrade Cipriani, I don't hate him; I'm just mortally afraid of him. I had a sister who was like a lily. He might have borne her with pride, lightly, on one hand, in the Corpus Christi procession. Instead . . ."

"He was a victim too, don't forget that. He was innocent, yet he accepted a lifetime of imprisonment."

Gelsomina's face grew cold and hard.

"Do you seriously believe he was innocent?" she asked.

"Lauretta believed it, didn't she? She even cried it aloud, at the trial, in front of the judges. It's in the record."

"My sister loved him, and went on loving him blindly till her last breath. But the truth, where she was concerned . . ."

"What truth?"

"I don't even know what to call the crime Luca committed against her."

112

Wooden clogs pattered to a halt at the doorway of the shop. A little old woman called Gelsomina in a voice like the squeak of a mouse.

"One moment," Gelsomina shouted back. "I'm coming." Before going into the shop she dried her eyes on her apron to hide the traces of her tears.

"I could easily prove to you," said Andrea, when she returned, "that on the night of the murder Luca wasn't anywhere near the place where it happened."

"He told you that himself, I suppose? And you believed him?"

"I've talked with two people who saw him that night standing near their house for a long time. He was alone."

"Why didn't they give evidence at the trial? If Luca was innocent, why did he let himself be convicted?"

"I don't know. There are a lot of other things I don't know. But I assure you, Gelsomina, I'll have no peace of mind until I find out what it is that people are trying to hide from me by refusing to speak."

"Can't you ask Luca himself? I thought you were friends."

"Even he prefers to say nothing."

The woman's face betrayed a mounting tension and fear. Andrea took pity on her.

"Look, Gelsomina," he said in an affectionate tone, "I'll tell you exactly how I came to take such an interest in this story. Then perhaps you'll trust me. Let's make a pact, shall we? Let's try to help each other understand."

"All that matters to you," said Gelsomina, "is finding

113

out about the murder; but even before the murder, my sister's fate was sealed."

"What do you mean?"

"I don't know how to explain it to you," Gelsomina said. "The party doesn't approve. My comrades think I'm just being superstitious."

"Do you mean to say you've brought this up at party meetings?"

"Yes, I have. I've got some old-fashioned ideas, my comrades tell me. They know I do my best for them. The party is my new family. But they criticize me all the same. They say you can't fight for the freedom of the working class and at the same time believe in witchcraft."

"You think Lauretta was bewitched? By whom?"

"I used to be certain of it. But now . . . Now I'm back where I started. I've given up trying to understand. The rusty old sword that I've carried in my heart for forty years is as much of a torment now as it was at the beginning. Every day, toward evening, a feeling of dread comes over me—I can't describe it. At night I have the most fearful dreams. When I think of poor Lauretta . . . Forgive me," she barely managed to add. Then she broke down and sobbed.

The long-repressed explosion left her gasping as if she were about to suffocate. After a time her sobs gave way to moans, to deep-drawn wails, and at last to floods of tears. Throughout it all she continued, with clasped hands and imploring gaze, to ask forgiveness for behavior so unworthy of a comrade. Andrea was at his wits' end, not knowing whether to go or stay, or how to help her. Meanwhile a little girl, black-clad and barefoot, had crept into the shop, bringing a small bottle to be refilled with olive oil.

"Gelsomina," she begged repeatedly.

"Come back later," Gelsomina finally managed to answer, taking care to keep out of sight. "Please sit down," she went on, turning to Andrea. "Don't go away. I couldn't bear for you to go just now. Where had we got to?"

"In my time," said Andrea, "it was very unusual for a girl from this village to get engaged to a Cisterna man. In fact, I seem to remember that here in Perticara it would have been considered a disgrace."

"Yes," said Gelsomina. "That started after Luca's trial and Lauretta's death. They even made up a proverb about it: 'Better fall into the well than into the Cistern.' But in the old days it used to be the other way around. There was plenty of marrying between the two villages. In Cisterna the men were reckoned the finer stock, and in Perticara the women. And they had many chances to meet, what with all the visiting back and forth on summer feast days; besides which, the poorer Perticara folk would often go to Cisterna as day laborers to pick up a little money. So naturally people got acquainted, and sometimes the acquaintance grew into a liking."

Gelsomina stood up, cleared the coffeepot and cups from the table, and put them in a basin on the floor.

"If it's not too painful for you," said Andrea, "tell me more about those days."

"When Lauretta and I were young girls, there was a very rich man in Cisterna, who dealt, among other things, in the wholesale fruit business. I wonder if you ever knew him later on? Don Silvio we called him."

"Silvio Ascia? Yes, I remember him vaguely."

"He used to buy up the local produce—walnuts and almonds chiefly—from all over this part of the country, and export it. Of course he made a handsome profit. He used to have as many as twenty girls working for him during the season, shelling the nuts and packing the crates for shipment. The girls were mostly between twelve and sixteen years old, and there were nearly always a few from Perticara. I was thirteen and Lauretta fifteen when we first went to work there. This Don Silvio wasn't a bad sort; sometimes he was even fairly generous, but every now and then, being rich, he had whims. We were starting home one evening, when, on the pretext of wanting to make sure we weren't sneaking out with stolen almonds in our bodices, he ordered us to parade in front of him, one by one, showing him our breasts. Most of us were still children, as I've told you, and we took the whole thing as a joke. But Lauretta seized my hand and refused for us both. When Don Silvio insisted, she said: 'Send for your wife, Donna Ortensia. Let her search us.' Just at that point, Luca appeared in the doorway. We didn't know him then. He'd come to load the crates that were ready, and take them to the railway station. With Luca present, Don Silvio didn't dare go any further. He got out of it by saying to Lauretta: 'Very well, since you're such a smart girl, I'll trust you.' But the next time Don Silvio tried the same trick, the other girls took their cue from Lauretta. 'So you think we're thieves? All right,' they told the boss, 'we're willing

116

to be searched, but only by your wife.' He shouted for a few minutes, but he wasn't really a bully, and finally he abandoned his lewd prank. Not long afterward, he and his wife gave a party, and Lauretta was the only one of the girls who worked for him whom he invited. Maybe he wanted to prove that he didn't bear her any grudge. He even told her she could bring me too. It was a Sunday afternoon in April, and glorious weather. Lauretta had a new dress that suited her to perfection—pale blue trimmed with pink. Mother pinned a red rose in her hair. She really looked a beauty. When we got to the party we found a lot of lively people. First we were given a fruit cordial and biscuits, and then, later on, ices. During the party Don Silvio introduced us to his wife, Donna Ortensia. Her reputation for oddness was borne out even at that first meeting. Did you ever know her?"

"Never. I think she died in some hospital when I was only two or three years old."

"She didn't die until much later—and it was a mental hospital. But even on the day of the party, we could see that she was mad. Wait till you hear. She took it into her head that Lauretta should dance with Luca, and when my sister refused—either because she was shy or because she didn't know much about dancing—Donna Ortensia insisted almost to the point of using force. After the dance she called my sister aside, vexed and red in the face, to tell her that she shouldn't have held her partner so close. You can imagine my poor sister's embarrassment. It upset her so much that she never danced another step as long as she lived. When the party was over and we were saying good-by, Don Silvio said: 'You don't propose walking all the way to Perticara?' 'Why not?' replied Lauretta. 'When we come for the almonds, we do it twice a day.' 'But today, you're my guests,' Don Silvio told her. 'I'll have Luca take you back in the buggy.' And so he did. The buggy had us home in a quarter of an hour. During the drive, Luca was very friendly and full of jokes, but in a well-mannered way. I remember that Lauretta never once opened her mouth, and left me to answer the few questions he asked us. When we reached home we found our parents sitting beside the door, getting a breath of fresh air. I don't recall now whether it was that time or the next that they asked Luca in for a glass of wine. At any rate, Don Silvio repeated the courtesy of having Lauretta driven home, even on ordinary working days. And since my sister wouldn't dream of going in the buggy by herself, she'd take me along with her, or if I wasn't there, some other girl from Perticara. It was always Luca who drove. That was how, gradually, they began to feel at ease with one another, and an understanding sprang up between them, even though they were never alone together for a moment. In those days, fond feelings could be expressed only in glances. Now it's all right, even here, for a girl to speak to a man in public, but at that time it would have been scandalous. The young man had to come to the girl's home, and her mother saw to it that they weren't left by themselves for one minute. But I must say that Luca didn't seem to mind such restrictions. He was a serious young man—reserved, withdrawn. The only fault we ever found with him was that he was often silent and thoughtful when he was with us, although,

118

according to what we heard, he was often very merry when he was at the tavern or with his friends. Sometimes my father would tease him. 'You're not worrying about all the bad things that haven't happened to you yet?' he'd say. But we really liked Luca all the better for being so reserved. Lauretta, of course, was devoted to him.''

"Did they become engaged right away?"

"Yes and no. He behaved as though they were engaged, but he held back from proposing. Lauretta obviously couldn't bring up the subject before he did. In the end it was Don Silvio who brought up the subject.''

"What business was it of his? Luca wasn't an orphan. And even if he had been, he wasn't a deaf mute.''

"That's pretty much what my father answered when Don Silvio took him aside, one market day, and said: 'Don't you think it's high time this marriage was settled?' As for Luca, he was very much put out when my father told him about it. All the same, it got them talking about it, and the talks finally led to the official betrothal. We gave a party to celebrate, and that was how we came to know Luca's mother, Teresa. . . . But I'd rather not say anything about her. May she rest in peace.''

"Why not? I wish you would tell me everything that's on your mind.''

"The least I can say is that Teresa wasn't straightforward with us. That same evening, soon after she got to our house, a woman arrived from Cisterna with a betrothal gift for Lauretta from Donna Ortensia. She opened the box and showed us a magnificent pair of gold earrings. Lauretta was as overcome as the rest of us. Nothing could have justified so inappropriately extravagant a gift from a woman who had so often been so rude to her. 'Everyone likes getting presents,' my sister said, 'poor people especially; but they have to come from the heart.' Therefore, she said she didn't feel that she could accept the earrings. But the Cisterna woman had such a wheedling tongue that it finally became impossible to go on refusing. Perhaps Don Silvio's wife had at times seemed a little impatient, she said. The gift was intended to prove how fond of Lauretta she really was. And a present that might seem extravagant to a poor girl might mean nothing at all to a rich woman. After all, she went on, the poor need someone to protect them. And so on and so forth, with more sugary words of the same kind, until finally Lauretta apologized for her original refusal."

"Who was this woman?"

"The miller's wife."

"Agnese?"

"Yes, indeed. Is she still alive? We'd known her for a long time. There was no electric mill in Perticara then, and we had to take our wheat to the mill at Cisterna. We'd heard she was some relative of Donna Ortensia. Certainly, she and her husband were in and out of that house all the time. They weren't the only ones, mind you; quite a number of people used to manage, in one way or another, to get good pickings from Don Silvio's household. So much so that when a few years later Donna Ortensia was locked up in the madhouse and Don Silvio went off to America, Cisterna fell on lean times. But forgive me, that's not what I meant to tell you about. Where were we? Oh yes, Teresa. Well, that first evening, when Donna Ortensia's present arrived, she, too, seemed to be strangely embarrassed. She helped persuade my sister not to refuse the gift, but while her arguments didn't make any particular impression on us then, later on they set us thinking. 'Don Silvio's wife is a capricious lady,' she said. 'She's got a good heart, but she sometimes does harm without meaning to. You're both very lucky,' she went on, 'to have Donna Ortensia's blessing on your betrothal.' 'We're very lucky,' Lauretta retorted, 'to be so pleased with it ourselves, and to have our parents' consent.' That was a good answer, wasn't it?"

"But how did Luca react to all this? What did he say?"

"As far as we could see, he was truly fond of Lauretta. If he hadn't been, he could have broken off the engagement at any moment. No one would have tried to hold him to it. But he too—I don't exactly know how to say it—he too was strange."

"How did he explain Donna Ortensia's present?"

"Her presents."

"There were others, you mean? And was it always Agnese who brought them?"

"Yes, and they were all really valuable—a necklace, two rings, another pair of earrings. Every time, Luca began by saying that they should be sent back. But then Agnese would pour out her muddled arguments, and he, too, would give in. He did stand firm on one point, though. 'Keep them if you like,' he told Lauretta. 'We can always sell them if we need the money. But I implore you never to wear them.' How often in the years that followed I remembered those words. Why couldn't Luca have warned us of the danger?"

"What danger?"

"Unfortunately, he was thinking only of himself. I don't suppose he was a bad man, really; but he was greedy and secretive. Lauretta locked the jewels away in a drawer. Neither of us ever dared to try them on; but sometimes we'd steal a look at them, in secret. We were so poor. We wanted at least to feast our eyes on them. They had a strange splendor. Even in the dark, they shone as though they were alive. We'd seen gold before, but none that shone so brightly. These glimpses always left us troubled and restless. We were relieved when finally several months went by without a visit from Agnese. We of course saw Teresa now and then, but they were tranquil meetings. It even looked as if Donna Ortensia had put us out of her mind. Our peace seemed assured."

"But what about the wedding? Was there still no talk of it?"

"Father spoke to Luca about it more than once. They'd been engaged for almost two years. Nothing unusual in that; long engagements were common enough in those days. On the other hand, what was the point of waiting? Each time, Luca seemed to agree; but he hesitated when it came to naming the actual day. Before getting married, he said, he wanted to buy a cart and a yoke of oxen. Then he must have a new house to bring his bride to, he said. He explained, on another occasion, how small and tumble-down the old one was."

"Were these just pretexts?"

"I don't think so. The way my father saw it, Luca's association with Don Silvio had gotten him used to too much good living; he could no longer put up with a poor man's existence. Well, the season arrived when there isn't much farm work to do, and people attend to their family affairs. My father thought he could force destiny's hand; instead he provoked catastrophe. He kept at it until he got everyone to agree to a reunion at our house for the purpose of deciding the wedding date. The property arrangements had already been made: Teresa was giving her son her house and vineyard and a certain amount of money. The strange thing was that this sum corresponded exactly to the amount taken from the murdered man."

"You mean that Teresa, to see her son married, was counting on that hold-up in advance? She'd have had to be out of her mind."

"I'm only telling you what happened, Comrade Cipriani. The amount of money was exactly the same in both cases. The whole story was full of such diabolical coincidences."

Gelsomina fell silent and buried her face in her hands, as if suddenly overcome with weariness.

"My God," she said after a little while. "My God, here I am, telling the story of that evening all over again. How many times have I told it in the last forty years? How many times will I have to tell it in Eternity?"

"If you're tired," said Andrea, "if you'd rather I came back later . . ."

"Don't leave me alone," she said. "Not now, I implore you. If you go away, I'll just sit here telling it to myself. That evening, Luca arrived at our house very late, long after all the relatives were assembled. Teresa had sent word asking to be excused; she wasn't feeling well. We'd

123

had snow earlier in the day; the night air was bitterly cold out, and the roads icy. Luca arrived on foot. He seemed keyed up, but we thought it only natural, considering his temperament. But when I took his hand, I almost screamed. It was like a hot iron. 'Are you sick?' I asked him. He smiled and shook his head. We cheered up when he sat down and asked for something to drink, which he didn't usually do. He gulped down several glasses of wine, one after the other. When Mother brought Lauretta into the room, he rose at once and bowed very low to her—as one does in church. We took it for a joke, and were just about to laugh, when it suddenly dawned on us that he was in earnest. He was trembling with emotion. At this point, in walked two musicians, engaged by Father to liven up the party. One played the accordion and the other the clarinet. At first Luca refused to sing for us, although we'd often heard that he knew some beautiful old ballads. In the end he did sing one, beautiful I grant you, but very sad and not at all suited to the occasion. It was about a soldier given up for dead, who comes home and finds his bride married to another man. When he finished he sat down by the hearth and fell completely silent. He just sat there, staring into the fire and poking the embers with the tongs. We were used to his changes of mood, but the rest of the company didn't think it very polite of the bridegroom to withdraw from the conversation. So Lauretta went and sat beside him, hoping to make him talk and draw him into the circle. For a long time Luca didn't respond to the friendly coaxing of his betrothed; he simply stared at her, as if he couldn't understand what she wanted. At

124

one point, he seized her hand and raised it to his lips, looking deep into her eyes. Once or twice he seemed about to speak, to reveal something, but he couldn't. Then: 'I despise myself,' he said. He looked as though his life was ebbing away. Finally he began to weep. He sobbed like a child. His face was filled with despair. Lauretta was terrified. 'I don't want you to be unhappy with me,' she told him. 'It's not too late to withdraw.' To everyone's amazement, Luca fell on his knees before her and begged her forgiveness for the pain he was causing her; then he turned to my parents, to me, to the guests and even to the musicians, begging forgiveness of us all. He was incoherent. 'I can't marry you,' he said to Lauretta. 'It would be a sacrilege.' Someone asked him what he meant. 'I mean a sin of the spirit,' he said. 'I am not worthy.' His face was unrecognizable. The rest of that night was a horror. Lauretta could not stop crying. 'What's to become of him?' she said between her sobs. 'What will happen to him now?' "

"In the record of the trial," said Andrea, "the testimony quotes Luca as saying, 'Forgive me, Lauretta, I am not worthy of you, I'm a criminal.' Did he really say those exact words? Can you remember?"

"He undoubtedly said something of the sort," Gelsomina replied. "Next morning—it was a Friday—we looked at one another as if a thunderbolt had fallen on the house during the night. 'My poor daughter,' Mother said to Lauretta, 'maybe you've had a lucky escape. Imagine what a life you'd have had, married to a man like that.' But Lauretta could only think of what would become of Luca.

'I hope nothing dreadful happens to him,' she kept repeating. 'May God protect him.' That afternoon one of the musicians brought us the news of Luca's arrest. It was an indescribable shock; but at the same time it cleared the air and put an end to our bewilderment. It was a Friday—did I tell you?"

"Yes, you told me; but does it matter?"

"Things don't happen by chance. Even if the party . . ."

"Lauretta never had any doubts about Luca's innocence?"

"Lauretta loved him. Some time afterward, the judge gave her permission to visit Luca in prison. The examining magistrate probably hoped that Luca would confide in her and tell her where he'd hidden the loot. I went with her as far as the prison gates. When she came out, the first thing she said to me was: 'Luca is innocent.' 'What makes you think that?' said I. 'Did he tell you so himself?' 'No,' she said. 'I looked into his eyes. Gelsomina, I swear to you that he's innocent.' That's how much she loved him."

"I think she was right," said Andrea.

"Father returned the presents to Don Silvio," Gelsomina went on. "They only met for a few moments, and neither of them spoke a word."

"There's no mention of Donna Ortensia in the record. I wonder why?"

"In this part of the world the law doesn't annoy the rich."

"Madness, apparently, is less considerate."

"My poor sister even had the courage to go into the witness box. She testified against her father and mother,

against me, against all her other relatives. We brought
forward proof of Luca's guilt; she denied it, and insisted
that his words had a wholly different meaning. But no
sooner was she back home than she took to her bed. One
evening . . ."

Gelsomina hesitated.

"Tell me everything you know," Andrea urged her.

"The party is against it," she said.

"Never mind the party. This is none of its business."

"None of its business . . . ?"

"You were telling me about Lauretta's illness," said
Andrea. "Go on."

"At first the doctor thought it was just an emotional
upset. Later he said something about heart disease. But
before she died Lauretta confessed to me, weeping, what
she had done. She had disobeyed Luca and one night, when
the rest of us were asleep, she had put on her prettiest dress
and decked herself out in the accursed earrings, rings and
necklace, and preened in front of the looking glass. She
thought she looked beautiful. She was still admiring her
own reflection, curtsying to it and paying it compliments,
when suddenly she saw Donna Ortensia standing behind
her, all dressed in red. She nearly died of fright, but she
had strength enough to make the sign of the cross. The
apparition vanished, and Lauretta believed she was safe.
But the curse had already laid hold on her."

CHAPTER ELEVEN

APPROACHING the old mill, Andrea had seen Agnese hanging up her laundry on a cord stretched between two poplar trees. But as soon as she caught sight of him she ran to the house and locked herself in. Andrea had been on the move ever since dawn, and for several days he had not shaved, so that he had a swarthy look and a threatening air.

"Open up!" he shouted, pounding his fist against the door. "I have something to say."

"My husband's not here," Agnese answered from inside.

"Never mind about him," said Andrea; "it's you I want to see."

"He told me not to let anyone in," she shouted back apologetically.

"I'm not here to seduce you," said Andrea. "Come along out!"

"Can't you come back another time?" Agnese implored him. "Today's Friday."

"I'll smash the door!" threatened Andrea.

Finally she let him in. She was looking even more untidy and timorous than usual.

"What is it?" she whimpered. "Do we have to start all over?"

"I've been to Perticara," Andrea told her. "I had a talk with Lauretta's sister, Gelsomina."

"Well, what about it? Have you come to tell me all your private affairs?"

"Doesn't the name of Lauretta mean anything to you? Once upon a time you used to go see her, and take her presents."

"I've always stuck strictly to my own business," said the old woman in a tremulous voice. "All I want is to be let alone."

Andrea sat down on a big stone near the door, as if to show that he didn't intend to go away. The growth of beard on his face accentuated its thinness, and his masterful manner filled Agnese with fear.

"A pleasant spot, this," he observed. And he added, mockingly: "Was it strictly your own business when you took Lauretta presents from Signora Ortensia?"

"Ortensia belonged to my family," said Agnese tartly. "I'm surprised you don't know that. She was my niece."

"Fine family feeling you showed her! Do I have to remind you what name is given people who act as go-betweens in illicit love affairs?"

"What do you mean?" she protested. "Luca and Lauretta were engaged to be married."

"And what was the relationship between Luca and Ortensia, may I ask?"

Agnese made a gesture of weariness and sat down on the doorstep. Suddenly she looked little and shrunken and very old.

"Dear Lord," she muttered. "Is there no end to this story?"

"Raise your head," said Andrea. "While you're talking, I want to look into your face and see what you're holding back."

"I'm not afraid of you," said Agnese, gazing out of her teary eyes straight into those of Andrea. "Don't think for a minute that I am."

For some time they stared at each other. The expression on Agnese's face was that of an obstinate child.

"Now that you've looked your fill," she said, "tell me what you have seen."

"I've seen that you have something to say," said Andrea, more gently than before, "and that it would do you good to say it. It's good for all of us to get something off our chest once in a while."

"What can I tell you that you don't already know?" said Agnese. "Ortensia was my sister's child, and all of us were very proud of her. Because Ludovico and I had no children, we loved her in a very special way. I'd have done anything for her sake."

"Were you the one that arranged her marriage to Don Silvio?"

"He was the best match for miles around."

"You mean he had the most money?"

"It wasn't the first time that a rich man took a fancy to a girl far below him on the social ladder."

"Gossip has it that your husband derived some financial gain from the marriage."

"We've always been like donkeys that carry wine on

their backs and drink nothing but water. But gossip can always find a target. Just now, people are saying all sorts of things about *you*. . . . If Don Silvio and my husband had various business dealings together, wasn't it right for them to share the profits?"

The old woman fell suddenly short of breath and had to pause for a moment's rest. There was something miserable and worn about her; she seemed like a whipped dog on a leash.

"There are more clothes that I must hang up to dry," she said beseechingly. "A whole basketful of them."

"Later on," said Andrea. "You've plenty of time. Meanwhile, tell me more. Unburden your conscience."

"I only wish I could," she said with a resigned sigh. "In spite of Don Silvio's wealth and Ortensia's poverty, I can truthfully tell you that they were in love. Don't go making a face at me! If you'd known my niece, you'd take my word for it. She was mischievous and impulsive, but she was also terribly proud. She would never have married merely for money, believe me, or to please her family, either."

"But when she got married, she had to break off her affair with Luca, didn't she?"

" 'Affair'? What do you mean? Fifty years ago, no one in these parts had ever heard such a word. I still don't know what it signifies."

"Luca and Ortensia had exchanged words with each other. . . ."

"Yes, but not promises. They smiled and spoke whenever they met. Perhaps just once, through a barred win-

131

dow, they clasped hands. That's all there was to it. As soon as Don Silvio entered the picture, Luca stepped out of it. In fact, he was invited to the wedding, and came."

"Didn't Ortensia and Luca dance together at the reception that followed?"

"None of those present criticized them for it. Large numbers of relatives and friends were present. And Ortensia had her husband's approval. . . ."

"But it seems that Luca was deeply stirred. . . ."

"Luca? Who in the world could understand him? Before she was married, he seemed indifferent toward her. Only afterward, did he show any real feeling. It was a painful sight; every time he caught a glimpse of her, he positively glowed. And yet, when he knew that Don Silvio and Ortensia were sacramentally bound together, he should have realized that he didn't have a chance with her any longer."

"Unfortunately, Ortensia had a way of reviving his hopes, periodically."

"Mind what you're saying!" the old woman interrupted with unexpected vigor. "You're speaking evil of the dead."

"I'm sorry," said Andrea. "I know that there's something hateful about what I'm doing."

"Oh you know it, do you? That's a point in your favor!"

"But look here, Agnese," he insisted. "You know perfectly well that your niece often let Luca come to her house. If a man's unwelcome, he can be snubbed or put out the door."

"You say that because it fits in with what happened later. But no one foresaw the tragedy at that time. I'm speaking to you just as if I were in the confessional; whatever I say now, I'm willing to repeat at God's judgment seat. Perhaps we, on our side, were foolish or careless. But the fault was really Luca's; you know that."

"I don't follow you. What fault do you mean?"

"Holy Mother of God! The fault we're talking about! There ought to be some difference between a man and an animal. When it's a question of his relations with a woman, a man knows that the answer is marriage. Signed, sealed, and that's all there is to it. Up here, to live means to sweat blood, every day of the year. Living's a dead serious matter; perhaps you didn't know. . . ."

"Well, for Luca too, marriage might have been the solution. If it hadn't been that Ortensia . . ."

"But Luca's marriage was first off Ortensia's idea. She was the first one to speak of it to Teresa and me. 'We must find him a girl,' she said. And when she let Don Silvio in on her little plan, he came up with Lauretta, the girl from Perticara, and said all sorts of good things about her. She may have deserved them, of course, but her parents . . ."

"They didn't want those presents you brought."

"Oh, they pretended to turn up their noses at them, but in the end they took them. The presents were really from Don Silvio; they were bought with his money. As soon as Lauretta's parents guessed that Luca had rich benefactors, their greed knew no bounds. Especially the mother's. 'My sweet girl hasn't any trousseau,' she complained to me. 'She hasn't the copper kitchenware or the two chests of drawers a bride is supposed to bring with her. . . . It isn't right that the bridegroom should only be obliged to provide a house and a couple of acres of land. A certain amount of cash ought to be required of him as well.' Even when it came to her harvest of walnuts and almonds, she claimed that Don Silvio ought to pay her more than he paid the other peasants."

All of a sudden Andrea interrupted: "Here comes Don Serafino!"

Without further delay he got up and went toward the row of poplars which separated the millstream from the yard around the mill. The old priest was perspiring and breathless; he had knotted a white handkerchief around his neck and carried a gray umbrella to protect himself against the sun.

"What's the matter?" he asked Agnese. "What can I do for you? You sent for me. . . ."

"What on earth for?" Agnese exclaimed with surprise. "I don't need the last sacraments, you can see that for yourself! . . . And Ludovico is perfectly well. He's gone to market. . . ."

"Just a little while ago, Toni came to my house to say that you wanted to see me as soon as possible."

At this moment he saw Andrea sitting on the grass, between the two poplar trees, and realized that a trick had been played upon him.

"You rascal!" he shouted, waving his umbrella threateningly in Andrea's direction. "You miserable schemer and racketeer! . . ."

"Go right on," whispered Agnese encouragingly. "Call him anything you like, and add a few names on my account, while you're at it."

Andrea laughed and beckoned to the priest to come closer.

"Come over here," he said. "It's cooler."

The spot was cooled not only by the shade of the poplars but by the freshness of the nearby stream. The poplars were tall and straight, the most beautiful in the entire countryside, and although the shadows they cast were slender, they were dense. The stream ran over a bed of brightly colored pebbles and its water was crystal clear. On the other side, a field of tall hemp raised a dark green wall, and beyond it, near a mass of reeds, two girls were washing clothes and laughing together.

"You really must forgive me," Andrea said to the priest. "At your house, Luca is always under foot, and you know that certain things can't be discussed in his presence. Sit down beside me and catch your breath. You didn't have to hurry."

"If it were up to me," panted Don Serafino, "I'd dispatch you both to a desert island. I've had quite enough of the pair of you, and I mean exactly what I say."

"What have we done that's wrong?"

"Nothing. That's the whole trouble. You're a pair of noble nuisances. No criminal has ever brought this neighborhood the trouble that must lie on Luca's conscience. If every generation produced a couple of innocents like Luca and yourself, there would be no more law and order."

"Sit down," Andrea repeated. "Law and order could also be called a whited sepulcher."

"You're not going to expound the Gospel to a priest, are you?" shouted Don Serafino, infuriated.

Agnese had sat down near the door of her house, with her head bent low and a general look of exhaustion. Finally, with an effort, she got up and went inside. Using the umbrella as if it were a cane, Don Serafino bent his knees and collapsed onto the grass beside Andrea. Lately he had begun to show his age. He had grown very thin and breathed with difficulty.

"Yes, this is a most agreeably cool spot," he said, somewhat reconciled. Then, pointing at the door through which Agnese had just disappeared, he added: "Have you been tormenting her again?"

"It's impossible to get anything out of her except with a sledge hammer," said Andrea apologetically.

"This morning you weren't to be seen," said the priest. "We were waiting for you. Were you pursuing your investigations? You have a real policeman's nose, there's no doubt about it."

"Trying to insult me, is that it? I thought the cool breeze had pacified you."

"No, I mean it. It's only natural that men who have been persecuted should develop an instinct for tracking other people down. Heaven help us when the persecuted come into power!"

"Well, if you must know, I did go by your house. But it was at a bad time. You were quarreling with Luca."

"You could have announced yourself, couldn't you? Or did you prefer listening at the door? I have found out that you're quite capable of it."

"It wasn't necessary. At certain moments you were shouting at the top of your lungs. I waited for a while, hoping it would blow over, and then finally I went away. How did it start?"

"It was all on your account."

"Yes, I gathered that much. That's why I got you to come up here."

"I'm afraid I hurt Luca's feelings," said the priest. "He wants to go home."

"To the ruins of his home, you mean?"

"You should try to calm him down. If he goes away, it will be very painful for me. Everyone would know about it."

"By the way," said Andrea. "There's something I must tell you right away. From what I overheard of your quarrel this morning, I gathered that not even you know everything about Luca's old trouble."

"But before you imagined I did? For once, your policeman's nose led you astray."

"You're leading me from one surprise to another," Andrea went on. "Let's think it out. The trial affected you in many ways, didn't it? It stirred your feelings, made you suffer and caused an upheaval in the parish that was in your care. How could you give up wanting to know the truth? No, don't give me a conventional reply. Just for once, let's have no hypocrisy."

"I knew all I wanted to know."

"And exactly what was that?"

"Just about as much as you know now."

"Is that all? Because I haven't yet got to the bottom of it."

"Oh well, only God knows that."

"Don Serafino, don't put me off with supernatural excuses," said Andrea impatiently. "I'm momentarily stuck at a certain point of the story. . . . Luca went away from Perticara about ten o'clock in the evening, heading toward Cisterna. He should have arrived there an hour later, but nobody witnessed his arrival. Or, tell me this: *do* you know of anyone that saw him there around eleven o'clock?"

"Nobody saw him."

"I'm not sure I ought to believe you. But let's go on from there. Four hours later, around three o'clock in the morning, Ludovico found Luca standing near his mill-race. Had he come there directly from Perticara? If not, where had he been in the meantime?"

"My poor fellow, can't you see that you're getting yourself into the field of spiritualism?"

"With all due respect for the dead," said Andrea, "don't you think he spent those hours with Signora Ortensia?"

"Ridiculous! If that were the case, the next chapter in the story wouldn't make sense."

"Why not?"

"Why should a man who was able to spend the night with his mistress let himself be sentenced to life imprisonment?"

"All right; go ahead," said Andrea. "Let's hear your version of the story."

"If Ortensia and Luca had been adulterous lovers, then, mind you, we should have had a comedy rather than a tragedy on our hands. I can speak of it quite frankly, because what I know I learned not in my priestly capacity, but rather as a friend and distant relation. Their confessor was the priest from Perticara, who came to say Mass in

138

our church almost every month. You see, for a number of years, all the feeling had been on one side. When Ortensia got married, she wasn't at all in love with Luca, even if she had joked and laughed with him. In other words, she knew Luca had a fancy for her, but she didn't suspect how strong it was. To all appearances, after her marriage, she was as vain and flirtatious as before, both with Luca and with all the other young men who had courted her when she was a girl. But in reality, believe me, she was the soul of honor. She was excitable, she rolled her eyes, talked in a loud voice and illogically, but if anyone said a word or made a gesture that offended her modesty, she put him in his place immediately.

"Of course, with Luca, she had no occasion to be severe. She had never imagined, any more than the rest of us, that he was capable of such unusual devotion. Before her marriage they may have exchanged a few tender words, but in all probability she quickly forgot them and did not dream that they were indelibly engraved in his heart. As a matter of fact, he never asked anything of her. He did not protest against her marriage, and it never occurred to him that she could break her marriage vows. But he didn't take into account the fact that, in a small place like this, so persistent and powerful a passion was bound, in the long run, to make for an intolerable situation. For love had poor Luca completely in its power. He was hard-working, courteous and cheerful as before, and yet anyone could see that he was thinking and dreaming of Ortensia all the time.

"Even at church, during the Sunday Mass, his eyes were

139

invariably fixed upon her. The result was that nobody followed the Mass: they all were watching those two. Finally I had to call him into the sacristy and give him a scolding. 'You must keep your eyes on the altar,' I told him, 'not on some woman.' The next Sunday he followed my admonition and looked straight ahead of him all the time, but this behavior was so unnatural on his part that he attracted the same attention as before. To make a long story short, I was forced to ask him to keep away from church and stay home.

"Every time the two of them met, even by chance, the same thing happened, and a morbid tension was built up between them. But their meetings weren't always the result of pure chance. There were certain family gatherings at which they couldn't help running into each other. You know that, in Cisterna, just as in every other small village, the ties of relationship are so complicated that everyone is more or less kin. And by now it was quite obvious that as soon as Ortensia appeared on the scene Luca was blind to everything else. If he had shown the least sign of insolence or aggression, then he would have been put in his place immediately. Instead, things became more and more serious, especially after we noticed that Ortensia was gradually responding to him. When he stood in one corner of a room, she drew him into her own circle. She asked him to air his views on every subject under discussion, as if nobody else inspired her with the same confidence and she considered him a peg above the rest."

"Was she very beautiful?"

"Yes, as far as I could see, she was, but I can't tell you in exactly what way. That was something people talked about quite a lot in those days. 'She's beautiful,' they said, 'but what's the real reason?' She was tall, and slim, with big greenish eyes and impeccably combed chestnut hair. When she smiled, she was lovely to look at, and she smiled frequently."

"In other words, her poor relatives looked on her as capital to be invested with extreme care."

"Yes, she was like a gold mine, or a lucky lottery number. There aren't so many ways of raising oneself from a life of poverty. And in our part of the world, a beautiful daughter has always been one of them. After she was twelve or thirteen years old, the whole family began to count on her good looks. She was brought up to cherish this aim, and she readily accepted it as a law of both nature and society, and one in which she could take due pride. Her manner was half bold, half innocent, and she was as superficial as beauty usually demands that a woman be.

"Marriage put more color in her cheeks and increased her beauty. But Luca held the traditional view that complete respect is due to the marriage vow. He accepted it and submitted to it completely. There was absolutely no reason to doubt his sense of honor. He did not even claim the right to talk about his love. Such talk is commonplace; it is on everyone's lips. But he gave his feelings no name. Since they concerned only himself, a name would not have added anything to them. And he had no idea of the fact that, in spite of this reticence, he was heading straight for disaster."

"You could have let him alone, since he wasn't doing any harm."

"Now you're talking like a man from the moon! This

isn't a village; as we've said before, it's a great tribe. We're all connected in one way or another, and no one's business is strictly his own. Gossip of the most incredible kind about the relationship between these two was the principal subject of every family conversation. The tribal tradition, as you know, has a sort of rustic chivalry about it: adultery calls for revenge by the knife. But Luca's behavior didn't fit the traditional pattern. He was altogether absurd. Your father, who was very fond of him, used to be angry. 'Go on to bed with her,' he said; 'that way it will soon be over.' Every time he saw him, he repeated: 'Go on to bed with her. Then you'll find out that she's just a woman like any other.' But Luca didn't want to talk about it. He broke with your father, simply because he didn't want to hear any more advice of this kind. In a way . . .''

"But Luca wasn't completely green," said Andrea. "Some of the men here who were in the army with him say that he wasn't above going to whorehouses."

"Oh yes, in that respect he was just like the others," admitted Don Serafino. "He was neither an angel nor subnormal. But this passion of his was out of the ordinary. It was an impossible love."

"A love that made no claim."

"A love that was totally absurd," said Don Serafino. "And with all of this, he was extraordinarily mild. Just the opposite of you."

"How do you mean?"

"He was milder and, at the same time, stronger."

"He was resigned, is that it?"

"No, he had greater assurance; he was single-minded.

You might hate him, but you couldn't pick a quarrel. He knew exactly what he wanted, and he was quite damnably stubborn about it. 'My feelings are not your concern,' he said to me once. I told him that from a Christian point of view, feelings concern me more than anything else, since sin lies in thoughts rather than in deeds. 'There's nothing I can do about it,' he answered. As for Ortensia, she wasn't cut from the same cloth. She was less stable, less secure; indeed, she was moving rapidly toward a state of hysteria. She became morbidly sensitive. I remember how, one day in the sacristy, the sight of a rose in a glass of water on my desk moved her to tears. 'You're ruining her,' I said to Luca; 'you're making her unhappy. Is that what you call love?' This was the only argument that really hit home and finally brought Luca around to accepting certain suggestions as to how the tenseness of the situation might be relieved."

"IIe could always have gone away, or emigrated."

"Yes, at one time there was some such idea. Luca had gotten a passport and put together the money for a steamship ticket. But on the eve of his departure, Ortensia stood in the way. 'As long as he's unmarried, I shall have no peace,' she said. 'We must find him a wife, to make him happy.' And so we held a sort of family gathering to discuss a marriage. How that failed you already know."

"No, I don't. I don't know a thing."

"Go along with you!" protested Don Serafino. "You know just as much as I do."

"No, I don't. And I'm not altogether convinced by what you say. How could you and Teresa and Ortensia allow

Luca to let himself be sentenced to the penitentiary? That was no joke! I'm sure that you knew something you didn't say."

"We knew that Luca was in a desperate and untenable situation. The penitentiary was a way out. Doesn't that satisfy you?"

"Not at all. Teresa would never have accepted such a solution. Can't you see that your explanation is as abstract as if it had come out of a psychology manual? You're still lying to me."

"Your insistence is getting on my nerves," said the priest, painfully raising himself off the ground. "I never thought that in the last days of my life I should have to put up with so much harassment."

CHAPTER TWELVE

"LUCA went to look for you in your lodgings," said Don Serafino. "Didn't you meet him on the way?"

"I went out by the garden gate, and left word to keep him there until I got back."

"You can't go on this way. He'll lose patience."

"I have a buggy today. My motorcycle is out of order. You'd better come along with me. I can take you for a very pleasant drive."

"No," said Don Serafino. "I don't want to make a fool of myself by being seen in your company."

"I need a couple of additional pieces for my puzzle. At this point, I'm unwilling to admit defeat."

"The more pieces you gather, the more confusion there'll be in your mind," the priest warned him. "It seems that the other night, a strange, spectral light was seen in the abandoned Ascia house. Just enough goings-on so that there was talk of ghosts and other such mischief. I suppose that you were at the bottom of the whole affair."

"Just recently, you mean? No, I was at Aquila, where I went to visit the district insane asylum."

"Did you get your head examined while you were there? I wonder they didn't lock you up."

"Nowhere in the records was there any trace of Signora Ortensia Ascia."

"Then she must have been taken somewhere else."

"Do you know where?"

"No."

"The town clerk told me. As a matter of fact, it's in the vital statistics, for anyone to see. Signora Ortensia Ascia died last year in the Benedictine convent of Saint Clare, atop San Rufino. I'm going there now."

"Do you want to lay flowers on her tomb?"

"I want to talk to the Mother Superior."

"Is that why you've put on a white shirt and a tie? I don't believe she'll talk to you, even so."

"Then I'll say that I've come in your name. After all, you were the one that sent Signora Ortensia there, after she'd lost her mind."

Just then Toni shouted up from the road: "The buggy is ready!"

"Good-by," Andrea said to the priest. "Shall I convey your regards to the Mother Superior?"

"Look here . . ." Don Serafino said brusquely.

"Have you changed your mind? Do you want to go along?"

"No. But there's a fact of considerable importance of which I wish to inform you. Sit down. The coffee's almost ready; I made it myself."

"Well, what's it all about? . . . At least you know how to make a pot of coffee. Congratulations!"

"When Signora Ortensia left her husband's house, she wasn't out of her mind."

"I'm not surprised. You drove her crazy, later on."

"No, she was never crazy at all. Only there was no other explanation we could give the local people for her sudden departure."

"You've got a poker face, all right!" exclaimed Andrea. "You told me you didn't know a thing, and all the time you had this up your sleeve."

"My respect for the secrets of men's souls is something you simply don't understand," the priest said dryly.

"No, frankly, coming from you, I don't. I consider it simply a way of preserving your peace of mind."

The priest closed his eyes, as if he were feeling slightly sick, and for some time he remained silent.

"Andrea," he said at last, in a low, resigned voice: "if you think you're talking to a man satisfied with the way he's faced the tremendous difficulties of his calling, then you're very much mistaken. Nobody knows better than myself my limitations and delinquencies and sins. But for the tragic end of Luca and Ortensia I don't feel that I'm to blame."

Don Serafino looked like the trunk of a felled tree. He had ceased trying to defend his position, and now he let himself go.

"The catastrophe was brought about by forces whose existence we didn't even suspect. There was no way in which we could intervene. When we heard that, under questioning, Luca had not defended himself against the charge of homicide, in spite of the fact that he was innocent, we

147

didn't know what to do. None of us had lost his mind, but over our rooftops we felt the blasts of a wind of collective folly. Those were terrible and agonizing days. Poor Teresa, Luca's mother, shut herself up in the church; for three whole nights she wept, in front of the Holy Sacrament, and would take no food. Ortensia was in a state of complete despair. She groaned, shouted, called upon God and Satan, accused herself of the most tremendous crimes, tore her hair and beat her head against the wall. One night Don Silvio summoned me to pronounce the prayers for the exorcism of evil spirits. I found before me a poor miserable creature, utterly bewildered and at times irrational. She wanted to go to the judge at once and testify on Luca's behalf. The carriage was ready at the door."

"Did she want to testify to facts which she alone knew?"

"We had a very hard time dissuading her. Then and there, we decided to try to gain time. The first thing to do, we told her, was to question Luca himself. After that, there were periods of alternate calm and anxiety, depending upon the news we had of Luca's attitude during the trial, when he would not agree to allow any testimony in his defense."

Don Serafino paused, in order to catch his breath.

"Go on," said Andrea. "You're over the hump now."

"There's no use my going through the whole trial," said the priest. "A few days after sentence had been pronounced, Ortensia sent for me. I found her alarmingly thin, a mere bag of skin and bones, but in a tranquil frame of mind. 'I've lost my blood, drop by drop,' she told me, 'ever since he's been in jail. Now I feel like a hollow shell.

If he has accepted life imprisonment for my sake,' she told me, 'I can't stay in this house. I can't help thinking of him all the time. There are stories of men who have died for love, but Luca is doing more than that, because the penitentiary is worse than death; it involves not just a moment of courage, but a lifetime of confinement. . . . Don't think that the sacrifice I intend to make will leave me unhappy. Quite the contrary. At last, I've found someone in whom I can believe. I believe in Luca. And how in the world am I to stay here? At this point, no one can accuse me of leaving my husband's house to run to the arms of my lover.'

"You can imagine how these words made me feel. Out of a sense of duty, I murmured something about the indissolubility of the marriage tie. But that was no longer the real question. Thanks to the violence Luca had practiced upon himself, Ortensia had recovered a liberty as precious and as total as that which he had lost. She had meditated for a long time upon the special nature of the shame which follows upon the sin of infidelity. Only in her case, the situation was the reverse of the usual. 'Who can deliver me from the shame of appearing at the Judgment Seat having abandoned the man who has pledged me his soul?' The woman in front of me was no longer the vapid, inconsequential creature I had known before, but one transformed by suffering. Life had mastered her, and she had become one with her fate. Have you ever seen a human being's naked soul?"

"What do you mean? A soul detached from the body? A ghost?"

"It was a marvelous and terrifying thing. For a moment all the conventions were swept away. I was completely incapable of preaching to her. The usual commonplaces died on my lips. And she could not be swerved from her decision. All she asked of me was that I explain things to her husband and family, and contrive, with them, to make up a plausible story. And so all those who had accepted Luca's conviction for a crime he did not commit had now to accept Ortensia's pretended madness. As a matter of fact, most of the family was genuinely persuaded that she was mad. Hadn't she been perfectly content with Don Silvio? Surely, in her life with him, nothing was lacking. Ortensia left the house by night. Her husband was nowhere to be seen. She appeared at the door, standing in the dim light of a lamp, as white and erect as a candle. Without casting a single look behind, she climbed into the carriage, where I was waiting. 'You must thank Silvio for me,' was all she said. 'Thank him for what?' I asked stupidly. 'For keeping out of the way.' "

"And how did her husband take it?"

"After his wife left, he went off to Brazil and bought a coffee plantation. His departure brought ruin to Cisterna. I think he must be still alive."

Once more Toni's voice came through the window.

"The buggy's ready. Do I have to let the horse stand in the hot sun?"

"Stay where you are; I'm coming," shouted Andrea.

A minute later he got into the buggy and set the horse to trotting. He drove along without paying much attention to the landscape. The road was empty and the whole countryside seemed uninhabited. While he drove, the sun reached its highest point in the sky; it was a sun against which there was no possible protection, and it seemed as if everything—mountains, trees, meadows, path and rushing streams—was revolving, on a spit, around it. At every curve in the road, the convent building appeared and disappeared. On the last steep ascent of the San Rufino Pass, the horse dropped into a walk, and Andrea jumped down to the ground. He wound the reins around the brake, and covered the final curves on foot, walking beside the buggy.

At last he came to a sort of plateau, where the old convent was situated. In front of it lay a grassy expanse, dotted with clumps of stones and bushes. There were no other buildings anywhere in sight, except two ramshackle, deserted houses, without either doors or windows. The convent itself was surrounded by an enclosed garden, whose walls were almost entirely covered with ivy. Andrea tied the horse to the gate, gave him a bag of oats, and walked up the main drive. The façade of the building was surfaced with cracking yellowish plaster, and the shutters at most of the windows were closed, giving it an abandoned air. Black crows flew low over the roof, cawing raucously. Near the entrance, an old man was raking the dry grass into heaps; he must have been either a deaf mute or a case of retarded development, for he did not answer Andrea's greeting. Andrea pulled the rope attached to a bell above the door, and after a long pause, when he was about to pull it again, the door opened, and a slight, wizened little nun, in black robes, appeared before him.

"I've been sent by the parish priest of Cisterna," said

151

Andrea. "And I have urgent business with the Mother Superior."

"Did you bring a letter from him?"

"No; it's something I can explain face to face."

"But you have no letter of introduction. What is it all about?"

"It concerns Signora Ortensia Ascia."

"Surely, you know that . . ."

"Yes, she died a year ago. . . ."

"Come in and sit down. I'll tell the Mother Superior, but I'm not at all sure that she'll see you."

Andrea followed her through a dark hallway to a courtyard, with a well in the middle. Another nun stood there, holding out a plate of birdseed to some doves. Her motions were so graceful that he paused to admire them.

"Come along," said his guide.

She led Andrea into a large drawing room, as dark and cool as a cellar. After she had thrown open a window giving onto a garden, Andrea saw that in one wall of the room there was a small aperture, covered with a grate, and in front of it an armchair was standing.

"Wait here," said the nun, "but, I repeat, I don't know that the Mother Superior can speak to you."

The armchair was the only piece of furniture in the room. On the high walls hung dark paintings: portraits of prelates and abbesses and benefactors, and romantic landscapes with sanctuaries. In the air there was a faint odor of mold and candle wax. In spite of the large size of the drawing room, it seemed doubtful that more than one visitor a year was admitted to it, and over all there hung a funereal calm. In the surrounding countryside people openly discussed the fact that the convent was on its last legs, and speculated as to what would become of it when the last nun was dead.

Andrea's wait dragged on, and in order to pass the time, he went over to the open window. It looked out on that part of the garden used for growing vegetables. An old nun was drawing water from a well and watering a bed of lettuce. At a certain moment, a bell rang in the distance, and the nun dropped her work and made the sign of the cross. Meanwhile, the sound of a door opening, somewhere behind the grated aperture, warned Andrea that the Mother Superior was near, and he went over to the grate. A white form moved in the darkness behind it, but it was impossible to make out facial lineaments, age, or expression.

"Sit down," said a soft, tenuous, disembodied voice. "Do you come from Cisterna? What is your name?"

"Andrea Cipriani."

"Cipriani? Years ago, we had a most generous benefactress from Cisterna, called Annamaria Cipriani."

"That was my grandmother, a very devout woman. She brought me here once, when I was a child, and the Mother Superior gave me some delicious pastries. The convent holds a special place in my memory."

"And we remember your grandmother by name in all our prayers for the dead."

"Yes, she was a very devout and good woman," said Andrea. "May she rest in peace! But she was the ruination of the family."

153

"How do you mean?"

"I mean from an economic point of view. At least, so my father always told me. She left what should have been her children's inheritance to the Church. All for the good of her soul, no doubt."

"Did you know Signora Ortensia?" asked the Mother Superior. "Did she too belong to your family?"

"At Cisterna, Reverend Mother, everyone is related to everyone else. But I was never personally acquainted with Signora Ortensia, because she went away before I was born. As for her story, I know that at first hand."

"Is Don Serafino still alive?"

"Yes, he's an old man, and a stubborn one. Almost mule-headed in his stubbornness, if I may be allowed to say so. He wanted to come with me today, in spite of the fact that he woke up this morning gasping for breath. I had a hard time persuading him to send me in his place. Among other things, anyone enjoys revisiting places he knew as a child."

"When we informed him that Signora Ortensia was dead, he never answered."

"I am honestly surprised. And yet I can assure you, Reverend Mother, that he was deeply interested in her fate. Naturally, with old age, his mind has lost some of its sharpness."

"Perhaps he's no longer in charge of the parish. That must be it. We made the mistake of addressing the letter to the parish priest of Cisterna."

"Yes, that explains everything, Reverend Mother. Don Franco, the present incumbent, is an up-to-date, sport-loving, optimistic kind of fellow. Ah well, don't let's talk about that. . . . Don Serafino did, somehow, get news of her death. In fact, he celebrated a votive Mass—if that's the correct thing to call it—for Signora Ortensia's soul."

"If he had ever answered our letter, we should have asked him how to dispose of some of her personal belongings. You know that she spent forty years among us. She shared our life, but always as a guest. She was a sort of 'volunteer' as they say; she did not belong to our Order."

"That would have been impossible, I suppose, since she was a married woman."

"In any case, her personal property remained her own, and we wanted Don Serafino's advice as to what to do about it. When we had no reply . . ."

"Forgive me for interrupting, Reverend Mother. . . . I don't want you to think that I am making this visit with any material aim in view."

"What, then, is your purpose?"

Although Andrea must have known that some such question was coming, he appeared highly embarrassed.

"Well, Reverend Mother, if I must tell you the truth . . . I should like to know how Signora Ortensia spent her time during all the long years she lived with you. Did she find peace and serenity within these walls? Was she ever tormented by remorse? Did she speak openly to you or to any of the other Sisters?"

"You say that Don Serafino sent you?"

"You see, Reverend Mother, something very serious has happened. I hope you will understand what I have to say. . . . A man, who for Signora Ortensia's sake let himself be

155

sentenced to life imprisonment, has come back to Cisterna."

"Luca Sabatini?"

All at once there was a note of trouble in the Mother Superior's limpid, detached voice.

"Do you know and remember his name?" Andrea exclaimed. "Yes, a few months ago, he was finally proved innocent. Immediately after, he came home."

A long silence followed.

"How is his health?" she asked. "Is there somebody to look after him?"

Now there was a definitely feminine tremor in her voice, which Andrea immediately perceived.

"He's living in Don Serafino's house," he hastened to assure her. "His long 'rest,' if one can call it that, didn't do him any harm. Yes, he's a truly splendid fellow! Don't you think that such a man goes far to redeem the honor of his sex?"

"Have the country people made their peace with him? That, I can tell you, was a matter very much on Signora Ortensia's mind. 'Perhaps someday he'll come back,' she used to say, 'but he'll be old and helpless, and nobody will help him.'"

"Don't worry about that, Reverend Mother. He has a few trusty friends. As long as we have a crust of bread, he'll get his share."

"Is he still as proud as when he was young?"

"In spite of his seventy-two years, he's younger in spirit than any of us. But he is also considerably milder than he used to be."

There was positive tenderness in the Mother Superior's voice.

156

"Is he not embittered? Not charged with rancor and hate?" she asked. "Are you quite sure? It would be only natural, after all. A lifetime of confinement, when a man has no religious vocation, no grace of God, even, must be almost more than he can endure."

"Luca's vocation was Ortensia," said Andrea. "Unfortunately it didn't have God's blessing. Reverend Mother, the interest you have shown in my friend emboldens me to make a suggestion at which I hope you will not look askance. Will you allow me to bring him here for a visit on any day convenient for you to receive him?"

"Here? To what purpose?"

"So that you may come to know him, and also that he may hear from your lips the things you have just told me about Signora Ortensia."

"I needn't remind you that this is a convent. . . ."

"Of course, Reverend Mother, you will place such limitations on his visit as your Rule demands. But perhaps nothing forbids his looking, at least from the garden, at the window of Signora Ortensia's cell. Or at the trees and flowers and mountains which came within her view. You would be doing a charitable deed, I can promise you. Just think how much joy it would give poor Signora Ortensia!"

The Mother Superior did not answer right away.

"If he were a rough or profane fellow, I shouldn't even mention it," Andrea insisted. "But you know from what Signora Ortensia told you that he's no ordinary man. Now he is an old man with white hair. Can you deny him this tardy consolation?"

"Very well. He may come," the Mother Superior said at last.

"When? Perhaps tomorrow?"

"Whenever he likes, as long as Don Serafino comes with him. And he is not to announce his name at the door. Don Serafino's name will be quite sufficient."

"And what if Don Serafino is not able to make so strenuous a trip?"

"Then we'll have to wait for a day when he feels stronger. . . . Meanwhile, you have reminded me that Signora Ortensia left something with us to be turned over to Luca Sabatini. Just wait a few seconds. . . ."

The Mother Superior's shadowy white form withdrew into the darkness of the adjacent room. Andrea heard doors open and close behind her. During her absence he became increasingly nervous. When at last she returned, she was bearing a bundle of papers in her hand. Andrea got up, half trembling, and went close to the grate.

"What have you got there?" he asked her.

"In the last eighteen years Signora Ortensia lost the use of her legs. She lay on a sort of chaise longue, which was placed, depending on the weather, either in the garden or on the veranda. There she spent her time doing embroidery or writing. In obedience to her confessor, she kept a personal diary, which she submitted to his censorship."

And, after a pause, the Mother Superior went on: "She wrote very slowly, reflecting for days over a single word or phrase. When she knew she was going to die she asked her confessor to allow her to leave me a certain number of pages. 'They are for Luca,' she told me. 'Shall I try to forward them to him, in the place where he is confined?' I asked her. 'No,' she said; 'he'll soon be free.' I must admit that I wasn't all sure of being able to keep my word. But now the Lord has given us another proof of His mercy. Signor Cipriani, I am most grateful for your visit. Forgive me if the papers are sealed. She put the wax seals on them with her own hand."

CHAPTER THIRTEEN

DON SERAFINO climbed the steep, almost vertical, wooden stairway leading to Andrea's room, and found him packing a suitcase.

"You're not going away, are you?" he asked. "Just when you could begin to take it easy? You don't know how to enjoy life, I'm afraid. And what are all these papers on the table? Have you, too, written a neo-realistic novel?"

Andrea burst out laughing.

"It's a novel, all right," he said, "but it's pure imagination. I didn't really write it, either. This is the stenographic record of Luca's trial."

The priest's face took on a serious expression.

"Poor judges!" he exclaimed.

"It's not their fault; it's the fault of their profession," answered Andrea. "It's impossible to achieve absolute justice, except when it's a simple case of an eye for an eye."

"As usual, you're exaggerating. If you go on like this, you'll end up an anarchist. Not all trials are like Luca's."

"Right. There's another trial, the most famous and most typical of all. . . . In talking with a priest it's almost mandatory to cite it as an example. . . . What was the official reason for the condemnation of Jesus Christ? You taught me in catechism class that it had very little to do with the real one."

"That's enough from you, young fellow! You have a blasphemous way of mingling the sacred and the profane."

Andrea nodded and smiled.

"It's not without a purpose," he said. "You, on the other hand, don't really believe in the Incarnation."

"Now you're just trying to spread confusion!" said the priest. "In every civilized community there are crimes . . . and punishment."

"Yes, but does the punishment always fit the crime, that's the question," said Andrea. "But I've argued quite enough with you already. Just tell me this. When Luca was a boy, was there anything about him that pointed to such a singular fate?"

"He was dreamy and introspective, that's about all I can say," the priest answered. "For that reason we used to think he was something of an idiot."

"But he was redeemed by love."

"Redeemed, you say? Lost, that's how I'd put it. Human love is a very tricky business."

"Don Serafino, I can't bear to hear you reason along the same lines as Don Franco."

"Well, I don't know what there is in those papers, but during the trial he acted like a real idiot, I can tell you. And as soon as word of this got around, the courtroom was crowded with fashionable people, looking for a bit of fun. The prosecutor questioned him often about his

161

private life. 'Begging your pardon,' said Luca, 'but it's no business of yours.' You can imagine the laughter. All during the interrogation, he stared at something on the wall, above the judge's head. 'What are you looking at?' the judge shouted at him. 'At Christ on the Cross,' Luca answered. 'Isn't that allowed?' 'You're supposed to look straight at the person who's speaking to you!' 'Begging your pardon,' said Luca, 'but *He's* speaking to me. Can't you make *Him* be quiet?'

"Yes, it was an absurd and frightening sight. At the end of the summing-up, the judge asked, as usual, whether the accused had anything to say before the jury retired to its deliberations. Luca moved his lips imperceptibly. 'Speak louder!' shouted the judge. But Luca only blushed with embarrassment. 'What's that you're saying?' the judge insisted. 'I'm asking God to forgive you,' was the reply.

"His passive resistance was terrifying. If he had cursed, stormed or threatened . . . but nothing could shake his calm. He denied being the murderer and then proceeded to look at the succession of witnesses who testified against him as if their testimony had no connection with him whatsoever. A few minutes after the sentence was pronounced I handed him a parcel of clothes sent by his mother. 'Cheer up!' he said to me. 'You wanted me to go away, didn't you? Well, I'm going. You didn't want to see me hanging about the streets of Cisterna any longer, isn't that right? Well, you won't see me for a long time.' "

"He was stronger than any of us," observed Andrea. "I should never have been so brave."

"I don't know," said Don Serafino. "Without meaning

to, he did a great deal of harm. But only God can be his judge."

"Every time I think of Luca," said Andrea, "I wonder where in the world such a man can have come from. His features and voice and even the way he walks are all characteristic of these parts, and yet . . ."

"Under that meek and mild appearance of his, there's an incredibly tough core. He's as hard as a steel blade."

"As the blade of a bread knife, I'd say," put in Andrea.

"Mind you, that's the weapon responsible for the greatest number of domestic tragedies," the priest reminded him.

"But in this case, Luca himself is the victim."

"At first glance, yes. But just think it over. To him the whole of life was a matter of submitting to social violence. But by accepting it, he escaped violence himself and imposed it upon others. That is why people here look so unkindly upon him."

"My God! What a life it turned out to be! He in the penitentiary, and she in the convent! . . ."

"Yes, he in the penitentiary, and she in the convent, with hundreds of miles between them! And at the same time they were closer together than any pair of lovers."

"From my point of view . . ."

"What can you answer to that? . . ."

"Nothing," said Andrea, biting his lip. "I said I didn't want to quarrel with you just when I'm about to leave. Must you really be going? If you see Luca please tell him that I'm off this evening."

Don Serafino went directly to his own house. Nowadays

he was no longer stopped at every step by someone seeking his aid or advice. Only a few peasants greeted him, and they did so with obvious embarrassment.

Luca was in his room upstairs. Several times Don Serafino went up, tiptoed down the hall and peered through the half-open door. But finding him immersed in the diary Andrea brought, the priest withdrew. Luca was sitting on the edge of the iron bedstead, and tears like those of a child were pouring down his cheeks. When Don Serafino finally saw that the reading was over, he went into the room and sat down beside him.

"Don't mind my crying," apologized Luca, smiling and drying his face. "This is the happiest moment of my life."

"I'm happy that it should have been granted you," said the priest, moved by the sight. "Don't ever imagine that a moment of happiness is a small thing. Happiness only exists in moments."

Luca could not speak for emotion, but he nodded assent.

"I only wonder," said the priest, "whether love for a woman justifies so much suffering."

"There's nothing else in life," answered Luca with conviction; "is there?"

Don Serafino looked at him in surprise.

"So all my catechizing served no purpose, did it?"

Luca did not catch the implications of his question, but he answered.

"It served to prepare me for confirmation. What other purpose could it have had?"

"You're totally irresponsible," said the priest, pretending to be disgusted. "As I see it, your whole attitude is diabolically impertinent. Your pretense of renunciation gave you poor Ortensia. Andrea fell under your spell before he even knew you. And that isn't all. You've gotten the best of the severest punishment our penal code allows, now that we no longer have the death penalty. If life imprisonment were abolished, too, there'd be no respect for the law."

After waiting a moment to see if his old mentor had any more complaints to make, Luca said with a smile: "Andrea's a fine fellow, isn't he? To have met him, even this late in my life, is the second great gift that fate has granted me. I can't hold any grudge against life, really. Where is Andrea now? What is he doing?"

"Most likely he's repairing his motorcycle." And after a moment Don Serafino added: "Yes, he's an honest man, but at times he's also a bad one."

"Bad? Do you really mean it?"

"Yes, I'm sorry to say it, but with you I have to be frank. He can be utterly pitiless, and even cruel."

"It's as though we weren't talking about the same person."

"Oh, he's different with you," the priest explained. "You make him feel shy."

"Feel shy?" echoed Luca, laughing aloud.

"He's cruel in a special way, of which we up here have no experience. . . . Oh, I forgot to tell you that he plans to leave for Rome this evening."

"What? He's going away?"

"Of course, his concerns lie elsewhere. Actually, he's stayed here too long."

Luca's moment of happiness seemed already over. His lips paled and began to tremble.

"I must see him before he goes," he murmured, getting to his feet.

Andrea was in front of his house, taking apart the motor of his motorcycle, when he saw Luca almost running toward him. He laid down the monkey wrench and went to meet him.

"I hear that you're going away," said Luca, trying to catch his breath. "It's only natural," he added.

"I have to return to Rome," explained Andrea. "But I'll be back for a holiday."

"Of course," said Luca, swallowing his saliva. "I only wanted to suggest that we have a short walk together."

"If that's it, then I can postpone my departure," answered Andrea, laughing.

They took the short cut over the hill, leading to Perticara. The deep-seated harmony which had grown up between them was evident in every detail of the way they walked and talked together. To a stranger's eye they might have passed for father and son, in spite of the difference in their social circumstances and the fact that Andrea was tall and thin, Luca more thickset, with heavier features. The evening air was mild and bright, shot through with a gold, autumnal haze. On the roof of the church, the first swallows were gathering for their annual migration. Luca gazed around him, with a mixture of tenderness and curiosity. As they proceeded along the path, he saw, for the first time since his return, Don Silvio's abandoned house. He did not try to change direction, but his step slowed. The columns on either side of the gate had lost their plaster, and the gate itself, eaten by rust, was bound by a large chain. Poppies, thistles and weeds of every kind had invaded the garden, and the porch was overgrown with honeysuckle and ivy. The windows were tightly closed, but many of the shutters were broken. As the two men went by, a black-and-white magpie, which had been perching on a balcony railing, flew off with a hoarse cry.

"I went through that house just last week," Andrea was saying.

"I know. But how did you get in?"

"I put a ladder up against the kitchen window and broke through the shutters. It wasn't too difficult, because the wood had already given way. The rooms are all empty. But there was a small portrait of Ortensia on the wall. I took it away with me. I will give it to you this evening before I leave."

Luca was taken aback and did not know what to say.

"Thank you," he stammered. And he added: "These last days I've been feeling some sort of resentment toward you. You'll have to forgive me."

"I realized that I was running the risk of hurting your feelings," said Andrea. "But I couldn't give up, just the same."

"I had a hiding place," said Luca, "which no outsider had ever penetrated. Does everyone? I just don't know. It's not only a matter of shyness or reserve. I always had the idea that if you talk about certain things, their meaning is distorted."

They walked on for a way, without talking. Luca's attitude toward Andrea had undergone a singular change, which was obvious in the way he looked at him and smiled. There was no longer any need of reticence between them.

"This is where Ortensia lived as a girl," Luca said, as they went by a mass of ruins. "Every evening, just before the Angelus, she came with a copper jug to fetch water from the well, down the hill. I waited for her halfway, hoping to see the smile which would haunt my memory every hour until the following day. Yes, my whole life was the hourly prolongation of her smile. . . . What would life be, without some silent accord with the one we love?"

His voice was quiet and serene.

"I envy you," said Andrea under his breath.

"You went to the court, too, I know," said Luca. "Did they let you see their record of the trial?"

"I even talked with the judge."

"You mean he's still alive?"

"Yes, he lives with his memories. He's still convinced that you committed the murder."

"That man's head must be stuffed with printed paper," said Luca. "Imagine his thinking he could frighten me by thumping his fist on the book he had in his hand. 'What have you got in that book that's so important?' I asked him. 'Your lucky lottery numbers?' 'No, this contains the articles of the law,' he told me. 'Good,' I said. 'Only it's too bad they can't go into a salad.' I wish you could have seen him then. He was as furious as if I'd slandered his ancestors. Of course, all his ideas of right and wrong came from those printed pages. 'Is there any article,' I asked him, 'that refers to a man who marries a woman he doesn't love instead of one he does?' 'No,' he replied. 'Such actions are outside the law's control; the law doesn't concern itself with feelings.' 'Very well,' I told him. 'My actions are outside the law's control, too; they're not covered by any of your articles, and I don't intend to tell you about them. They're strictly my business.' "

At this point the path opened into the rough road which led upward, in broad curves, to Perticara. Here the two men met a wagon loaded so high with hay that the oxen pulling it could barely be seen. At their appearance, the man sitting on top of the load hid himself quickly, so that only the tip of his head was visible, and the wagon gave the effect of a stack of hay moving under its own power. They walked for a hundred yards or so behind it, and then took a narrow path, which wound among small fields and rocky outcroppings. Luca had taken off his jacket and swung it over one shoulder.

"It's hot," he said.

But he may simply not have wanted to go about the countryside looking like a landed gentleman. The path was deserted, for the work of harvesting vegetables and hay had drawn the peasants to fields far below. Andrea suited his pace to Luca's, who had to pause every so often to catch his breath.

"Why didn't you go away?" Andrea asked all of a sudden. "Apparently at one time you had your passport all ready. In those days, as you know, many men from

169

around here went off to the Americas. In fact, many of them stayed there and made themselves new, less difficult lives."

"People blamed Ortensia," Luca replied, "but they were wrong. When everything was ready, I realized that I absolutely could not live so far away. I felt as if I were only half a human being; she was the other half. This feeling was so strong that I couldn't repress it. Of course, I very rarely saw her, and we never exchanged a word except in the presence of others. Yet to live in the same village and within her orbit was the very least I felt entitled to."

Andrea started to object, but he did not dare to. At this point the path passed by an abandoned hayloft.

"Let's stop for just a minute," Luca proposed. "I'm not yet used to such long walks."

They sat on the trunk of a tree which lay on the ground under the roof of the loft. A hole dug into the ground, flanked by two stones, had served as a fireplace. Luca lit his pipe. The sun was about to set. From beneath a cloud emerged a sheaf of bright, golden rays, like those of a saint's halo. Every now and then, Luca inhaled a mouthful of smoke and gazed with serene blue eyes at the terraced fields and vineyards below. Because of his age and in order to rest better, he sat bent over, his elbows on his knees. Nevertheless, his gaunt features were still regular and forceful, like those of a granite statue, the brows strong, the eyes deep-set. He looked like a peasant resting at the end of his day's work.

"Do you see that clump of trees over there?" Luca asked. "All around it were my vineyards. My mother had to sell them to pay the lawyers. How many times, in these past years, I have dreamed of hoeing the earth or harvesting the grapes!"

Andrea was watching him without appearing to. Luca seemed melancholy, but serene.

"The Mother Superior was anxious to find out from me whether you had come back with any bitterness in your heart," he said.

"Toward whom should I feel bitter?" Luca replied. "Toward myself?"

Before their eyes there lay several hundred small fields, ranging in color through all the shades of yellow and red, and dotted by occasional spots of green. They were divided by low hedges or uneven stone walls, plowed in irregular furrows, running down the hill, and connected by criss-crossing paths. To the peasants, each field was identified by an ancient family name. The setting sun gilded the branches of the almond trees and threw a rosy light over the prickly hedges and stone walls.

"Look at that thatch hut," said Luca, delighting in the familiar landmarks. He knew every bush, ditch, clod and stone, and each one, like a beloved household god, made his eyes gleam with emotion. From where they sat, they could also see the village of Perticara, straddling the crest of the hill.

"I was up there last week," said Andrea, making a gesture in its direction.

"How was Gelsomina?" asked Luca. "At the trial she raged against me like a fury. Does she still hate me?"

"She's still afraid," Andrea told him. "And she still wears mourning for her sister."

"Lauretta was a really good girl," said Luca, "one of the old-fashioned kind. If I hadn't loved someone else, she'd have made me an ideal wife. But a man can't love one woman and have children by another. They would be bastards."

"Did you meet Ortensia before you went to Lauretta's house that evening?" Andrea asked hesitantly.

"Yes, I talked to her," Luca answered. "How do you know? Who told you?"

"I don't know," said Andrea; "I was just asking."

"It was meant to be a farewell visit," Luca went on. "Ortensia, as you know, was urging me to marry. I wanted to tell her that the wedding date would be decided that evening. Because she was the one who wanted it, I was willing to make that sacrifice. I knew that I might end up by going mad, but I had to assure her peace of mind and put an end to the village gossip. This was my intention.

"I must tell you that during the winter the front door of the Ascia house was always closed. One entered by a small back door, near the storeroom. That may have been why nobody saw me. I hoped to find Ortensia's husband with her; we had a little matter of carting to discuss. Instead, she was alone. 'Silvio's gone to the café, for his usual game with Don Serafino,' she told me. 'I have an important question to ask you,' I said brusquely. 'And because my whole future hangs on your reply, I beg you to think before you answer. The question is this: Do you really want me to get married?'

172

"Ortensia burst into tears at my question, and answered me with these words, which have kept me company for forty years: 'No, Luca, I can't want it, because I love you more every day. Only there's nothing I can promise you.' 'I'm not asking you for anything,' I said, falling at her knees. 'If I have your heart, that's all I need.' She helped me to rise and put her arms around me. It was the first embrace I ever had from her. (It was also the last.) At that moment I was flooded with an immense joy, such as I had never known. It was a kind of ecstasy. All feelings of uncertainty or fear were gone. Can you tell me what happens inside one's soul at such moments? All of a sudden, the whole world wears a different face. If I had seen horses flying through the air it wouldn't have surprised me in the least. You must forgive me, Andrea. I know I am talking nonsense. But you, too, must have been, at least once, in love. Does love always work just this way? Good Lord, all creation looked different. There was heaven in my heart. Hundreds of stars exploded in my head. Happiness had entered into my being and kindled a light there I had never guessed at. The whole earth seemed to be revolving around us two, like a top.

"When I found myself outdoors again, I remembered that I was supposed to go to Perticara. I was already late. I was supposed to go there to decide the wedding date. It seemed to me a strange, senseless obligation, taken on in another existence. I was stunned. I walked like an automaton. My one concern was to avoid being even later. And so I ran. I ran to my own doom. I took this same shortcut, although in winter it's dangerous. The holes in the path and the ditches were piled high with drifted snow. More than once I sank into it. My one anxiety was not to be too late.

"But when I was face to face with Lauretta and her family, gathered together to celebrate the occasion, I could hardly stand on my feet. The walls and floor of the room shook under my feet as if in an earthquake. Every joint in my body was mortally tired. My heart was heavy as a stone. I realized that fate had tricked me. I was like a mouse in the trap. Every affectionate word that Lauretta spoke increased my feeling of discomfort and guilt. In my despair, I talked wildly, I know. At the trial, the prosecutor said this was evidence of anticipatory remorse for the murder I had not yet committed. When I left Perticara, I was sure I would never live to see the next day."

"It was just barely ten o'clock," Andrea said, "still early in the evening. Forgive my asking, but you need not answer: Did you go back to see Ortensia?"

"No," Luca answered promptly. "What kind of a question is that? Haven't you understood anything about the state I was in?"

"Please forgive me."

"It wouldn't have been possible," Luca insisted. "I'm not talking about a physical impossibility, but a mental one. When I came out of Lauretta's house, I felt annihilated, as if the mountain had fallen on my head. I didn't believe I could go on living."

"Where did you spend the time between ten at night and three in the morning?" Andrea asked. "Did you simply wander about the countryside?"

"I can't give you an exact answer," said Luca. "I was half dead, I tell you. I have only a couple of memories with no connection between them. It seems that, without intending it, I even performed a miracle."

Andrea did not immediately catch on to what he meant. Luca pointed to a little chapel perched above a mountain gully.

"Have you ever been up there?" he asked.

On the mountainside, behind the chapel, there was a sheepfold. Moving around antlike inside it were a number of shepherds and their sheep. The chapel itself looked like a toy from a Christmas manger.

"I went there once when I was a boy; in those days it was the goal of a yearly pilgrimage," said Andrea. "I don't know if it still is."

"I want to tell you about a fresco on one wall," said Luca. "The chapel, as you know, is consecrated to Saint Gabriel of Our Lady of Sorrows. That evening, without knowing why, I climbed up to it. Perhaps because, a few years before, someone had committed suicide by throwing himself into the gully. The night was clear and cold. When I arrived at the top, sweating and exhausted, I heard a sort of lament coming from inside the chapel. You may remember that there is no door. 'Who's there?' I shouted. On the threshold appeared a woman in rags, a beggar, who had been praying before going to sleep. We all knew her. In summer, she slept in the ditches beside the fields; in winter in haylofts or on church porches. The first oddity was that, when I saw her, I remembered, in spite of my bewildered state, that I had a thousand lire in my pocket.

They had been lent me by Don Silvio, to buy a vineyard before my wedding. Since I believed I was about to die, I had no further use for them. 'Take it,' I said to the woman, pressing the banknote into her hand. In those days it was a considerable sum of money. I don't know that she instantly realized how much it was, but I remember that she thanked me over and over again. 'God bless you!' she repeated. The second oddity was that, thanks to some unknown instinct, I realized I could not throw myself into the gully before this poor creature's eyes. Perhaps I was worried about frightening her."

"Now I remember the fresco where your good deed is pictured," said Andrea, smiling. A beggar is receiving money straight from the hands of Saint Gabriel."

"So Don Serafino has told me," said Luca. "That, apparently, was my beggar woman's version of what had happened. One thing is sure: both saints and devils were abroad that night in our valley."

"And so Don Serafino knows both versions?"

"He knows everything, the sacred story and the profane."

"Scratch one story, and you're sure to find another," Andrea said. "How is anyone to know which one is true?"

"I know this: that in these last weeks you've given Don Serafino considerable pain. You mustn't judge him so harshly."

"You're right. He's a good fellow."

"He's more than that," said Luca. "When you know him well, you'll find he's a great deal more."

Several donkeys, barrels swung across their backs,

crossed in front of the hayloft, followed by their masters. The men turned their faces aside as they passed by.

"Once upon a time," said Luca, after they had gone on, "even strangers greeted one another when they met."

"But we're not strangers," Andrea retorted.

"I am concerned on your account," Luca said. "I am hurting your political career."

"It's a relief to me," Andrea said, laughing. "This way they won't be asking for any more letters of recommendation."

The sun had set. The two men got up to go back. But they did not want to take the same path. The new one they took was no more than a cattle track. Luca breathed deeply, with real satisfaction. Because they were going downhill, he was able to talk with less effort.

"I don't know why some people think cow dung has a bad smell," he said.

"They have different noses," Andrea explained. . . . "When you came down the mountain that night you probably took this very path."

"Probably," Luca said, "but I don't remember. I was unaware how the time went by, what I did and whether anyone saw me, or else I forgot. I don't know why I didn't carry out my plan to kill myself when I came to the canal. I must have stayed there for a couple of hours, staring into the running water. So they told me, and it's probably true. Despair had reached the roots of my soul and paralyzed it. I could not tell night from day. A few hours later, when I realized that I was in the hands of the police, I felt a sense of relief. For a little while, there was no need to exercise any will of my own. They'll make my decisions for me, I thought. I had emerged unharmed from an abyss of horror and desperation; nothing remained but absolute exhaustion. My interrogaters made me laugh when they threatened me with jail. Not even the threat of hell would have frightened me. The days went by, without my keeping track of them. My being arrested had provided me with a way out, an alternative to suicide. What could I do against fate, except allow it to accomplish its ends?"

As the two men reached the footbridge near the weir, they paused for a few minutes to watch the flow of the water. There was still a pleasant freshness in the air.

"I must admit," Luca continued, "that at that point I didn't foresee that my prison sentence would be so long and painful to endure. I don't want to talk about the ten years of solitary confinement. To talk about them I should have to think about them again, and it would be too painful. If there were a brain operation which could uproot from my mind the memory of those ten terrible years of living burial I should submit to it without hesitation. I can only say this, unless you already know it: that there's a greater difference between solitary confinement and ordinary imprisonment than there is between ordinary imprisonment and complete freedom. I came out of it brutalized. I felt more like a donkey or a mule than a man. That was the state I was in when I received the first letter from my mother, or rather from you, telling me about Ortensia, how she had left Don Silvio and sought refuge in a solitary place, and still cherished me."

"Was it Ortensia whom your mother referred to as

Verdina?" interrupted Andrea. "How stupid I was not to think of that! When your mother dictated those letters to me, she spoke only of her and of her thoughts of you. And I never guessed who it was."

"Nobody could have understood," said Luca. "I called her that as a child, because of her green eyes. Even my mother had never heard that pet name. It must have been Ortensia who suggested her using it in order to guard our secret. Despite prison and solitary confinement, that letter had a miraculous effect upon me. Suddenly I found myself in the state of ecstasy I had known after our last meeting, before I was arrested. I felt within me the superhuman power of love, the prodigious peace of perfect accord between two loving hearts. The distance separating us was painful, but it was a pain of love. I couldn't even hate my prison, since my having accepted it had revealed to Ortensia the strength and nature of my feelings and had resulted in her breaking the unnatural bond which tied her to her husband."

Andrea and Luca walked on in silence until they reached the outskirts of the village. Dusk had fallen, and the first lights had gone on. Animals were returning to their stables, chimneys smoked because housewives were cooking their evening soup, and crickets chirped beneath the acacias.

"It's late," Luca apologized.

"What does that matter?" Andrea said. "I'll leave tomorrow."

They crossed the square in front of the abandoned church of San Bartolommeo and sat down on the stone bench beside the door.

"It was then that I began to think seriously about getting out of prison," Luca went on. "Ortensia did what she could, from the convent, to help me; she put a lawyer and a monsignore on the job. After all, I had been sentenced for a crime I didn't commit. But justice is a pitiless machine and one which will brook no trifling. As soon as I heard that it was again a question of articles of the law, I knew it was hopeless. According to article so-and-so, paragraph so-and-so, the lawyer said, there could be no retrial without new evidence. And where is the new evidence, he asked me. There's no need of anything new, I answered; surely the original fact of my innocence should be enough, the fact that I didn't kill that man. That means nothing whatever to the law, he insisted; there's got to be new evidence. Well, I lost patience. I want nothing to do with the law, I told him. Actually, there *was* something new, but it didn't concern the law or the lawyers."

"What exactly do you mean?" asked Andrea.

"I mean Ortensia's new circumstances," Luca explained. "I thought of going straight to the King. Courts have to abide by the book, I said to myself, but the King can be guided by his conscience."

"You wanted to tell the King your whole story?"

"Not at all. If he had been willing to receive me, I should have asked him just one question: 'Do you agree that a man of honor can tell no one, not even the King's own court of law, certain things relating to his honor and the honor of the woman he loves?' I'm quite sure the King would have seen it my way. Without any reference to articles and paragraphs, he would have ordered them to set me free."

"There's something I'd forgotten," Andrea murmured under his breath. "We did have a King."

"But how was I to reach him?" Luca asked. "That gave me a lot to think about. By letter? I had already written, without effect. Then one day I remembered that the officer of the court in charge of all trials was called 'Prosecutor for the Crown.' With a title like that, I thought, he must have access to the King. But how was I to obtain from him the introduction I so much wanted? After writing him several letters which he didn't answer, I realized that my only hope was a new trial, I mean a trial for some new offense. What year could that have been? I don't remember, but it was when I was at Porto Longone, I am sure of that. The warden there wasn't such a bad fellow. When we had complaints to make, he listened, and because he had very fine teeth, he often smiled. Anyhow, I went to him one day, apologized for the offense I was about to inflict upon him and then gave him such a sharp right to the jaw that he fell to the ground. The damage was much worse than I had intended, because the fine teeth turned out to be false, and he spat them out on the floor like a handful of white kidney beans. How was I to know that, I ask you?

"But the worst was yet to come, with the crown prosecutor. The fight I had with him was a real one. As respectfully as possible, I tried to explain to him the reason for my attack on the warden and to persuade him to arrange an appointment for me with the King, at whatever time and place might be most convenient for him. And do you

181

know what answer that fool gave me? He had in his hand a book filled from cover to cover with articles and paragraphs of the law, and he tried to point out to me the ones that applied to my new crime. 'You can keep your numbers to yourself,' I said as agreeably as I could. 'I wouldn't know what to do with them.' "

"In the end, you struck him, too," put in Andrea.

"I simply had to. . . . But how do you know that?"

"It's all set down in the explanation of their refusal to grant you a pardon at the end of the thirtieth year of your imprisonment."

By now it was completely dark around them.

"What time can it be?" asked Andrea. "I feel as if I were awaking from a long dream."

Luca smiled, and two men got up and started to walk home. Hidden among the leaves of an acacia tree, a cricket repeated his monotonous chirp, calling for his tardy mate. In the whitened sky above Perticara rose a moon in its first quarter, yellow as a slice of overripe melon. The silent alley still held the day's heat. The only signs of life were the animals stirring in their stalls.

"The more I think about it," said Andrea, "the more I believe that quite a few people here in Cisterna knew you had nothing to do with the holdup."

"Everyone knew I wasn't a murderer, of that I'm quite sure," said Luca, "except, of course, the police. How else can you explain the bitterness some of the old folk still feel toward me? When there were still brigands in these mountains (that is, when I was a boy), more than one man took to the woods, and committed highway robbery and murder. And the general run of the population had a kindly feeling for these outlaws. But my crime, in peasant eyes, was of a different and more reprehensible character."

At the other end of the alley, a boy suddenly appeared.

"There's Toni," said Andrea. "He must have been looking for us all evening."

"Look here," said Luca, putting a hand on Andrea's arm. "You ought to do something for him. You ought to take him to Rome and see that he learns a trade."

"I'd thought of that already," said Andrea. "But if he goes, you'll find yourself very much alone among these people."

"I've never been afraid of them," Luca said with a smile. "And, besides, I haven't much longer to live."

Set in Linotype Scotch
Format by Robert Cheney
Manufactured by The Haddon Craftsmen, Inc.
Published by HARPER & BROTHERS, *New York*